Dear Dr...

Thank you
for everything.
You are the
best... on so
many levels.

Sincerely,
Bill

Soul Witness

Soul Witness

William C. Costopoulos

Library of Congress Control Number:		2015905169
ISBN:	Hardcover	978-1-5035-5838-0
	Softcover	978-1-5035-5839-7
	eBook	978-1-5035-5840-3

Print information available on the last page.

Rev. date: 04/08/2015

To order additional copies of this book, contact:
Xlibris
1-888-795-4274
www.Xlibris.com
Orders@Xlibris.com
708812

CONTENTS

Dedicated to my two beloved grandsons,
Liam DiFilippo and James McLaughlin,
for the joy they bring to my life.

ACKNOWLEDGMENTS

THIS BOOK COULD not have been written without the tireless effort of Nicholas Ressetar, my friend and law clerk for over thirty years. He did all the research and word processing and encouraged me throughout. Thank you, Nick.

Special thanks to Tanya S. Wagner who worked days and throughout many nights editing the manuscript. I had no idea how much work was needed until I saw her corrections in red . . . there was red on every page. Tanya is not only a technician but also a special person. Thank you, Tanya.

I want to thank my law partners—David Foster, Leslie Fields, George Matangos, and Heidi Eakin—for their patience and support. Writing can be a distraction, and it makes me moody, but they deal with it.

I want to thank Tiffany Lenda who typed and retyped the proposed versions, which were never final, and she also did not hesitate to inject her thoughts, but that is Tiffany. I also want to thank Jayme King for running the law office and my life, which required a lot of juggling and tolerance.

Thank you, John Bolan, for the title *Soul Witness*.

Thanks to Jill, my wife, for her insights and for always being there for me. Thank you, Kara, Khristina, and Callista—my daughters and inspiration—for calling me once in a while.

* Much of the research regarding historic events in this novel was generated by Nick from Wikipedia. It is with deep appreciation to this archive of information that this attribution is made.

PROLOGUE

STARING AT THEIR screens in disbelief, millions across the world watched a shocking video. An American reporter was struggling to get off his knees as the black-hooded killer sawed at his neck with a knife. The defenseless victim, clad in orange, was being beheaded. His name was James Foley.

The date was August 19, 2014, and terror in the world was taken to the digital level.

On September 3, 2014, another journalist, Stephen Sotloff, was also beheaded for the world to see. He too, clad in orange, struggled to get off his knees when the hooded executioner cut off his head in barbaric fashion. The executioner, known as Jihadi John, spoke with a British accent in a chilling, menacing tone. "I'm back, Obama, and I'm back because of your arrogant foreign policy toward the Islamic State and your insistence on continuing your bombings. Just as your missiles continue to strike our people, our knives will continue to strike the necks of your people."

The United States and the British prime minister David Cameron confirmed the authenticity of the video, and the Free World went on high alert.

Within days, a law enforcement bulletin went into immediate circulation, warning that Islamic State fighters have increased calls for "lone wolves" to bring their war and hatred to American soil. The bulletin emphasized that this tactic of radicalizing individuals, psychotic or not, was a significant threat to this country and that those who believed otherwise had better think again. Of the different types of terrorist structures, lone wolves were the most difficult to apprehend. Commanders and cadres and armies, because of their corporate structure, were capable of the most damage, but because of their organization, they were the easiest to identify. Lone wolves, on the other hand, because they act alone, with or without direction, brought terrorism to another level. The memo emphasized that America's military was strong abroad, but we have never faced the consequences of a lone wolf strategy or an internal mass revolt.

Real wolves move in the night and are deadly predators, gnashing their teeth and baring their fangs. They attack without notice— sometimes alone, sometimes in packs coming from all directions—and the end for their prey is always a bloody, painful death. The lone wolf memo declaring that ISIS was unleashing "lone wolves" on to American soil was a warning to their intended prey—the American people. The recent video release by ISIS of their beheadings was their howl, and it was heard around the world.

* * *

September 10, 2014

President Barack Obama, dressed in a dark blue suit and solid blue tie, took to the podium to address the American people and the world. It was a prime-time speech for America's response to the beheadings and promised terror by the Islamic State, known as ISIS. No one believed that this was a political move by President Obama. Both parties in Congress were united and supportive. His presentation was prereleased to the House and Senate, and his endorsement was unanimous. The president began his address as follows:

> My fellow Americans, tonight I want to speak to you about what the United States will do with our friends and allies to degrade and ultimately destroy the terrorist group known as ISIS.

> As commander in chief, my highest priority is the security of the American people. Over the last several years, we have consistently taken the fight to terrorists who threaten our country. We took out Osama bin

Laden and much of al-Qaeda's leadership in Afghanistan and Pakistan. We've targeted al-Qaeda's affiliate in Yemen and recently eliminated the top commander of its affiliate in Somalia. We've done so while bringing more than 140,000 American troops home from Iraq and drawing down our forces in Afghanistan, where our combat mission will end later this year. Thanks to our military and counterterrorism professionals, America is safer.

The president continued in his prepared remarks with calm and assurance, and his signature articulate cadence never wavered. He made it clear that ISIS is not "Islamic," for no religion condones the killing of innocents, and the vast majority of their victims have been Muslim. He described that organization as a former al-Qaeda affiliate in Iraq that has taken advantage of sectarian strife and Syria's civil war to gain territory on both sides of the Iraq-Syria border.

He impressed upon his captive audience, mesmerized by the subject matter, that these terrorists are unique in their brutality. They execute captured prisoners. They kill children. They enslave, rape, and force women into marriage. They threaten with genocide. President Obama promised that we will degrade and ultimately destroy these savages through a comprehensive and sustained counterterrorism strategy.

CHAPTER 1

BLACK FRIDAY

November 28, 2014
Macy's Department Store
Manhattan, New York

IT WAS THE Friday after Thanksgiving, known in the retail world as Black Friday, the busiest shopping day of the year.

At 9:00 a.m., Macy's Thirty-Fourth Street Department Store on Herald Square in Midtown Manhattan was bustling with anxious shoppers taking advantage of the sales, discounts, and huge inventory. The towering Christmas tree on the first floor was decorated with blinking lights and red ribbon and adorned with a star. The walls garlanded with tinsel and wreaths and the sound of Christmas carols resonating in every department added to the festivity and frenzy. Cash, credit cards, debit cards, prepaid cards, electronic transactions, prepaid checks, layaways, and deferred-interest financing were being processed at every counter.

Christmas was four weeks away, and there was no time to waste. Outside, the streets of Manhattan were already crowded. Subways were jammed with more shoppers, cabs were lined up at every terminal, and buses were filled to capacity. Wall Street would be open until 1:00 p.m. Business was good, the economy was back on track, and with the election recently over, it was politics as usual.

And then it happened.

At exactly 9:15 a.m., the first bomb detonated on the first floor of Macy's, shattering windows and glass counters and human lives. A series of three more bombs exploded in quick succession: one more on the first floor, another on the second floor, and a final one on the fourth. The elevators went into lockdown, the escalators stopped, and the screams and panic triggered predictable pandemonium. Those who were not killed or seriously injured rushed to fight each other for the exits.

The familiar sirens of fire trucks blared from every direction. Every ambulance in the city was summoned to Herald Square. Police cruisers rushed in with armored personnel carriers, and SWAT teams arrived within moments. Within seventeen minutes of the explosions, the streets of Manhattan were teeming with black-uniformed operatives carrying AK-47s. New York was an experienced city, having lived through the horror of September 11, 2001. Forever known as 9/11, that was the day when two commercial airliners struck the World Trade Center towers at the hands of al-Qaeda terrorists, the day when another commercial airliner struck the Pentagon, when a fourth commercial airliner, destined for the White House, crashed in Somerset County, Pennsylvania, all of which claimed the lives of over three thousand innocent people. Yes, New York City was, indeed, an experienced city.

But nothing can prepare a city for the heartache and anguish that such evil can bring when loved ones are lost to such barbarism. A mother carrying her lifeless child from the fire and debris of a bombed building is not something one gets used to, no matter the city's or a person's history. To witness such an event is hell . . . To experience it is unspeakable.

And on that Black Friday, in Midtown Manhattan, the unspeakable was visited on a devastating number of innocent people—mothers, fathers, wives, husbands, the elderly and young, and too many children shopping for Christmas with their moms and dads. Their cries and screams could be heard throughout Manhattan . . . and the echoes would be heard in the darkness for years to come.

The statistics from the bombing at Macy's were staggering. Of the one hundred and five people killed, thirty-two were children. Two hundred and forty were taken to intensive care, while scores more were treated and released.

The official investigation, known as MACBOMB, resulted in FBI agents conducting over thirty thousand interviews, amassing 3.5 short tons (3.2 t) of evidence and collecting nearly one billion pieces of information.

The result?

No arrests, no identified suspects. No one even claimed responsibility.

Most of the 2.5 million who attended the Macy's Thanksgiving Day parade just the day before breathed a sigh of relief.

CHAPTER 2

OUT OF CONTROL

February 9, 2015, 1:30 a.m.
Harrisburg, Pennsylvania

THOUSANDS OF SHIVERING people stood in the bitter cold on a hilltop in Lemoyne, Pennsylvania, known as Negley Park, to watch the roaring fire across the Susquehanna River consume a city block at the base of Pennsylvania's majestic Capitol Building. Thousands more watched from the west bank of that river as the relentless flames spread from one building to the next on State Street, and though the observers were separated by the wide river, the detonation of two bombs was deafening and frightening.

The fire started at about 9:00 p.m. on February 8, 2015, in the office and apartment buildings closest to the expansive steps of the Capitol. The historic brick and wooden buildings burned quickly, and in spite of the quick and heroic response of Harrisburg's fire departments, with support from all departments in the contiguous counties—Cumberland, Lebanon, Lancaster, York, and Perry—the fire continued to rage. Its spread was aided by the city's use of wood as a predominant building material in the early 1900s. The strong wind from the northwest carried burning debris everywhere, and within one square mile of State Street, an evacuation was ordered. Too many of those buildings in Downtown Harrisburg were topped with highly flammable tarred and shingled roofs. A major contributing factor to the fire's rage was a meteorological phenomenon known as a "fire whirl." As overheated air rises, it comes into contact with cooler air and begins to spin like a tornado. Those whirls on the night in question, with temperatures near zero, propelled glowing hot embers into the sky, with torchlike flames threatening the West Shore before falling into the Susquehanna River.

By daylight, Pennsylvania's National Guard had arrived with tanks and trucks for security, support, and cleanup. Helicopters from the Pennsylvania State Police barracks and the First Army hovered overhead. Crime-scene tape, barricades, and armed law enforcement personnel turned Pennsylvania's capital into a military takeover scene. The federal courthouse and the Capitol Complex were secured in rapid succession.

Because most of the buildings on State Street had been converted to offices, and two of them were Catholic churches, the death and injury toll was limited. Eleven apartment dwellers died, fifteen were taken to Baltimore's intensive care unit, and twenty-two first responders were treated and released. The preliminary investigation indicated that the fire was intentionally set, remnants of a single bomb were taken into custody by the Federal Bureau of Investigation arson unit, and throughout the night, fire drones were activated by the CIA on a picture-taking mission.

The official investigation, taken over by the federal government's antiterrorist agency, was known as CAPFIRE. It resulted in eighteen thousand interviews, many of which in Syria and Iraq; 2.7 short tons of evidence; and the collection of eight hundred million pieces of information. The fire and explosion destroyed or damaged eighteen buildings, all within one block of State Street; eleven burned to the ground. Together with the destruction of two parked cars, the cost of damages was conservatively estimated at $500 million.

The forensics bomb analysts confirmed that the perpetrators had used plastic jugs containing ammonium nitrate pills, liquid nitromethane, electric blasting caps, and high-octane gasoline that fed the fire from a crude, remote-activated pump. The source of these materials could not be determined.

On March 12, 2015, the United States Attorney's Office in Downtown Harrisburg received an open letter claiming to be from ISIS, and the letter asserted that this fire on State Street was set by eight lone wolves who were radicalized individuals from Pennsylvania. The letter further asserted that the original intended target was the United States federal courthouse on Walnut Street, Harrisburg, Pennsylvania, but that plan had been aborted. The letter's claim was dismissed as fraudulent based on its vague and erroneous details.

What wasn't dismissed was the fear and anxiety that the American people would now awake to in the morning and go to bed with each night. It was like a cancer, malignant and malicious, coming from diseased cells that were spreading through the bloodstream of a civilized society. The letter's claim may have been fraudulent and filled with inaccuracies, but the message in it was loud and clear . . . Evil was being delivered to America and was upon them.

The investigation continued with intensity and was universal in scope, for the tremor was felt throughout the entire Free World.

The result?

No arrests made.

No suspects.

No persons of interest identified.

CHAPTER 3

UNITED STATES ATTORNEY'S OFFICE

March 12, 2015
U.S. Attorney's Office
Harrisburg, Pennsylvania

T HE UNITED STATES attorney for the Middle District Samuel T. Nelson sat at the head of his conference room table on the second floor of the federal courthouse in Downtown Harrisburg. He was reading, once again, the letter dated March 12, 2015, and claiming responsibility for the State Street bombing and fire. His most trusted first assistant prosecutor Fran Korsakov sat to his right, and two of their most experienced FBI agents were in attendance.

A high-ranking contingent from Washington DC had made the two-hour journey to discuss this local investigation, which had national and international implications, and their unspoken intention was to make sure there were no screwups. Indeed, the director of the FBI counterterrorism division Liam Spokane insisted on being there and brought with him his own FBI agent, an FBI computer specialist, a CIA field agent, and a Muslim confidential informant. His entourage was never introduced by name.

Nelson both welcomed and needed the assistance that Washington DC was providing but reluctantly understood that he was directed (as opposed to being asked) by the attorney general of the United States to work with them. He was also directed to provide the Washington contingent with all information generated by the investigation at his end and to share his office's most classified findings and conclusions. Nelson was convinced that the sharing was not going to be a two-way street, and he was absolutely right.

This was not a Pennsylvania drug bust or a paper trail followed to uncover public corruption or tax evasion. The bombing and fire on State Street was believed to be an act of terrorism and war on the United States, something Liam Spokane was convinced the boys in Harrisburg knew nothing about.

Everyone there at the meeting, however, was a professional, and the palpable tension and sensitivity everyone was feeling would not be acknowledged.

Samuel Nelson was the appointed United States attorney for the Middle District and had been so for fifteen years, and his territory included all of Central Pennsylvania, with offices in Scranton, Williamsport, Lewisburg, and Harrisburg. He was fifty years old, with thinning white hair, which aged him by a decade, and gaunt because of his smoking but a legal tactician and skilled with the media. He enjoyed his press conferences, and now for the first time in fifteen years, he'd have a chance to perform on the world stage.

He would try this case personally because if there ever were an indictment, this would be the one to secure his legacy. He would try the case with his first assistant Fran Korsakov, who had been trying cases in that office since law school (1970, Dickinson School of Law, Carlisle, Pennsylvania) and was the undisputed master litigator in the Middle District and in the Eastern and Western Districts.

"I assume we all agree that this letter claiming responsibility is fraudulent," Nelson began, looking around the table for approval. He got it, for everybody shook their heads in affirmation.

"That having been said, I do believe this bombing and fire was the act of one lone wolf or more, possibly paid for and directed by ISIS, but maybe not. What happened is too aligned with the promises of ISIS and too close on the heels of the Macy's Black Friday bombings. I've already talked to the United States attorney in New York, John Rivero, and we've compared our forensic bombing results. Although the detonation devices were very different—his were more sophisticated—neither one of us can get around the timing, sequence of events, and the two soft targets. Does anybody care to comment?" Nelson asked, looking right at Spokane.

Liam Spokane didn't want to say a word but as a courtesy simply commented that it was too soon but said it with diplomacy and not demeaning in tone. Liam Spokane knew more about terrorism and antiterrorism than everyone in that room put together. He had served as a marine officer in Iraq during the "shock and awe" period of President George W. Bush and Saddam Hussein's capture and execution. Though that battle was one-sided, the visuals were horrific and forever engraved on his soul. He also did a tour as an advisor and intelligence officer in Afghanistan and suffered nothing but frustration from witnessing atrocities on both sides of the aisle.

Spokane was a man of few words, and though in his midfifties, he had maintained his sculpted body by working out in his private, well-equipped gym at home. As a former wrestler during his Purdue University days, he was still at his trim college weight of 177 pounds. His head was shaved, and the shrapnel scar on his right cheek, the result of an Iraq land mine, gave him a very tough and rugged appearance . . . not unsightly, just tough and rugged. That look was not softened by his tailor-made suits, mostly double-breasted.

Spokane's entourage held their breath, for they knew he was unpredictable when it came to tact and cooperation. His CIA field agent Nick Gregaros had served with Liam in Afghanistan and couldn't wait for this meeting to be over. His FBI computer specialist was a middle-aged, but very attractive, brunette. At thirty-five, she had already been vetted and cleared for ten years for the highest-level security access. She knew more about computers, coding and decoding, accessing and creating viruses, than anyone in Central Intelligence, the FBI, or the United States Armed Services. She took her work very seriously as she did her sexuality. She was not introduced, but her name was Yvette Lewis, and even her marital status and background was off-limits. Throughout the meeting, Yvette was expressionless . . . no read for anyone . . . nothing . . . like ice.

The Muslim confidential informant knew the drill; he was to say nothing, even if asked. The same instructions were understood by Liam's handpicked FBI agent, though this guy never had to be told.

"Well," Nelson continued after a long pause, "I understand that it may be too soon, but I really want justice here. I'll assume any role and do whatever it takes to get it. I'll turn over everything I have and would appreciate some reciprocity."

Spokane responded to the reciprocity request, and again, his response was controlled but clear. "We'll cooperate, Sam, but we do have constraints that I'm sure you understand. Before we leave, please turn over every photo taken by the drones on the night of the bombings and fire. I believe there were over a thousand. We also request the stills and footage from all security cameras that might be in possession of the Capitol police or the city of Harrisburg in addition to every photo taken by every media outlet and all television footage. If you've collected any selfies, we want them as well."

With that, the meeting was over.

After the Washington contingent had left, Sam Nelson looked at his most trusted loyal staffers still in the conference room and said, "That was bullshit."

Nobody responded, for they knew what just happened. Though Sam was affectionately known in the legal community as Samson, everybody knew that he didn't feel like Samson that day.

CHAPTER 4

CIA

June 4, 2015
Central Intelligence Agency
Langley, Virginia

SA GEORGE YODER had been handpicked by Liam Spokane for two reasons: he could be trusted, and he was detail-oriented to a fault, if there is such a thing as too much detail in counterterrorism assignments. Yoder was an alumnus of Stanford Law School and had graduated with honors in 1985. He looked as though he had been born and raised in a library . . . and still lived there.

Spokane also noted that this agent had no other life. He was single, had never married, had no children, had no hobbies or extracurricular activities, and did not date. Yoder's work was his life, and work he did, around the clock and always on call. He needed no direction or guidance, for he knew what the mission was. His appearance marked him as a nerd: he dressed the part, wore horn-rimmed glasses, and parted his blond hair neatly to the side . . . in other words, no pretenses.

Spokane had no interest in the bodyguard type, and Yoder fit the bill.

Since that awkward meeting in Harrisburg on March 12, Special Agent Yoder had locked himself in his office and rarely came out. Spokane and Yvette would occasionally interrupt him to see how he was doing or if he needed anything. Yoder would simply nod his head yes or no in response to both inquiries and go back to poring over everything on his desk, sometimes with a magnifying glass, sometimes with a powered looking glass, like one would examine a diamond.

* * *

The weather in the east, certainly in Harrisburg and in Washington that February, was piercingly cold. On the night of the State Street conflagration, the temperature was near zero. The trees and shrubbery were barren, sidewalks and steps were salted everywhere, and the blustery winds and snowfalls throughout the winter were bone-chilling.

The investigation into terrorism and ISIS since the Macy's bombings on Black Friday, and well before that, was headed by the division of counterterrorism in Washington DC. Liam Spokane would spare neither expense nor manpower. The country continued to bomb ISIS targets, and while there would be no boots on the ground, there would be plenty of intelligence gathering and sharing.

Spokane was no fan of sharing information and made that clear to the president of the United States and all generals of all armed forces in the field. He simply trusted no one, for he had seen such trust misplaced in the past, and that misplacement in his world had always resulted in tragic consequences. His Muslim informant was a classic example, for that young man was a son of Osama bin Laden, and that descendancy was instrumental in bringing about his father's death.

Spokane was once asked if he trusted the informant.

"No" was all Spokane said.

In his desire to get around the legitimate concerns of the country's military leaders in the field and the directive of the president of the United States but still share his information at least with them, Spokane would often keep what he knew to himself until it was time for action. That was a very risky tactic, especially when Congress would demand answers; however, if no one knew what he knew, there could be no embarrassment or harm to those above him.

The harsh winter finally departed, and in Harrisburg and Washington, spring was in full bloom. The cherry trees that ring the tidal basin in the nation's capital were radiant in their pink and white splendor. Surrounding Harrisburg's Capitol Building, the mature oak trees offered shade to the well-manicured curtilage. Coats, hats, and gloves were no longer needed, with temperatures ranging from the mild seventies to the warm nineties.

WILLIAM C. COSTOPOULOS

State Street was still under major construction, with demolition of the ravaged street still in progress. And though the seasons had changed, it seemed to Spokane that one reality in particular had not. With all his king's horses and men, and full coffers, the investigation into Black Friday and the investigation into the Harrisburg burning were producing nothing, absolutely nothing . . . not even a lead. His confidential informant kept returning to the United States undercover without providing a trace of evidence or even a rumor.

It really annoyed Spokane when he would hear from both United States attorneys in New York and Harrisburg, inquiring whether there were any developments. His annoyance got to the point where he could not contain himself, and finally, they stopped calling.

And then Yvette walked into his office and told him that Yoder would like to see him.

Yoder never wanted to see Liam Spokane unless there was something worthwhile to see him about, and Spokane's heart started to race. Yvette was excited to carry that message, but she knew that she would not be attending this conference.

* * *

If Spokane was a hard read, Yoder was impossible.

He walked into Spokane's ornate office and made eye contact with his boss, and impassive as he was, it was obvious this agent had come up with something significant enough to ask for this private moment. Yoder, who never wore a tie, had his crumpled checkered jacket on and his white oxford shirt buttoned to the top.

"I may be on to something, boss," Yoder said, without excitement or urgency but with unmistakable sincerity.

"You know I'm listening, George," Spokane answered. "I'm really listening."

"I've been in my office day and night for months going over thousands of photographs, but finally, there was one taken by a drone that got my attention. It was the shadow of a man watching State Street burn from the top step going into the front of the Capitol. He was beside a statue . . . wasn't hiding . . . But it was just odd. He was very much in harm's way, but it didn't seem to matter, and he was alone," Yoder said.

Spokane gestured for Yoder to continue.

"I had that photograph digitally enhanced by our IT guys, and when I got a better look at him, I knew I had seen him before . . . somewhere . . . There was just something about him that I remembered. It was back on September 11, 2001 . . . I wasn't working for you then, but I was assigned to that case, which included a review of all the picture-taking done at that site.

"The picture of him I remember from that site was not one taken by our government. It was one taken by the *New York Times* and published in an editorial, taken on the day those planes crashed into the towers. It was a picture of St. Nicholas Greek Orthodox Church that stood across Liberty Street from the World Trade Center in New York City. Boss, that church was completely destroyed in the September 11 attacks when the south tower collapsed. The small and humble church was the only house of worship destroyed in the terrorist attacks that day. It was the only non–World Trade Center building to be immediately destroyed although others were severely damaged, specifically, the Deutsche Bank Building and Fiterman Hall.

"The image of that church," Yoder continued, "which was very small, with the cross on the steeple in the shadow of the World Trade Center, was one to remember, but I especially remember the photograph of that lone individual standing on the steps of that church at a time after the planes hit but before the tower collapsed. That photograph depicts the same man who was on the top step of our Capitol entrance watching State Street burn."

Spokane did not know what to say. He was incredulous, for whatever this meant, but he knew they were on to something.

"Look at these two photographs side by side," Yoder continued and placed them before Liam Spokane.

And there was no doubt.

The silence in that room said it all, but Yoder, and Yoder alone, already knew what his next move would be.

CHAPTER 5

TRUST NO ONE

June 5, 2015

YVETTE LEWIS WAS brought into the loop but no one else.
Not the United States attorney in New York.

Not the United States attorney in Harrisburg.

Not the president of the United States.

Not the generals in the field.

Not yet, at least.

The man depicted in the photo on the steps of the Greek church on September 11, 2001, and on the steps of the Capitol in Harrisburg as State Street burned on February 9, 2015, was clearly the same. He was in his late forties and white and looked to be American or British. He was clean-shaven, and his hair was dark, swept back, and graying at the temples . . . and in both photos, he appeared to be observing the events of terror and horror very closely.

Yvette's computer-generated recreation of the man put him at 172 pounds, 5 feet 11 inches in height. In both photos, he had been casually dressed and hatless. In New York, he was wearing blue jeans, dress boots, a white shirt open at the collar, and a silk tan sport coat. In Harrisburg, he was wearing blue jeans, dress boots, a black cashmere coat, and black leather gloves.

Yvette had already gone into computer mode with access to photos of every potential terrorist suspect in the world. Her bank of photos was vast, but her search engine was state-of-the-art, and in less than an hour, she confirmed there was no match.

She virtual-shaved the suspect's head using her software, fitted him with various beard styles, tried different mustaches, performed plastic surgery . . . no match.

"Are you surprised?" Yoder asked her.

"Disappointed," she answered.

Yoder nodded in agreement.

Yvette had a soft spot for Yoder; he wasn't her type, but she liked him a lot. She was sure that he sensed it but never gave a hint.

She also was loyal to the United States government and a tireless worker, but unlike Yoder, she had a private life. She was a 2002 graduate of Bucknell University, a prestigious small Division I school in Lewisburg, Pennsylvania. It was expensive, but with her father well entrenched in the Wall Street hedge-fund world, money was not an issue. Nor would it ever be, for she was an only child. She had majored in computer science and was gifted with the intelligence needed to succeed in that world. She had minored in religion and studied the Old and New Testaments, as well as other major religions.

She could have been a model, but that was never her dream. She wanted to make a difference, and the intelligence division of the United States government, namely counterterrorism, gave her that opportunity.

Liam Spokane could have picked any computer analyst of the many on the government's payroll. He selected her, and while she knew she was qualified, she was also convinced that her perfect ass had something to do with it. He never said that, but she knew.

Early in Yvette's career in Washington, she met a young field agent for the CIA who actually was her type—a maverick persona, rugged, with an athletic build, and on the move. They lived together for years before they tied the knot, and while their romance was fast and furious and his assignments overseas may have kept the passion alive, it did bring about periods of loneliness that she did not enjoy. Into the marriage was born a son, now five years old, and because of her schedule and with a husband overseas, they had hired a much-needed nanny. Her husband's name was James Donegal Lewis, and her beloved son was Jimmy.

"Now what?" Yvette asked Yoder.

"What nationality do you think this guy is in the photo?" Yoder responded.

"I believe he's British. The computer has determined he's either American or British but favors the British conclusion," she answered.

Agent Yoder went into deep thought, seemingly forever to Yvette, and finally asked her to go into the archives and get him the entire history of the July 7, 2007, London bombings. He wanted the official and classified reports, all photos, all media coverage, photos and footage, and any information on the aftermath.

* * *

June 10, 2015

Because there was now an identifiable suspect, Yoder's tedious, self-imposed assignment moved more quickly. It was a long shot, but this academic agent had a theory.

On July 7, 2007, there was a series of coordinated suicide attacks in Central London, which targeted civilians using the public transport system during the morning rush hour. This fateful day in England was known throughout the world as 7/7.

On the morning of Thursday, July 7, 2007, four male British Islamists had detonated four bombs—three in quick succession aboard London Underground trains across the city and later a fourth on a double-decker bus in Tavistock Square. The four bombers self-destructed, but they also killed fifty-two civilians and over seven hundred more were injured in the attacks. It was the worst terrorist incident in the United Kingdom since 1988, when the tragic crash of PanAm Flight 103 known as the Lockerbie bombing, a suicide attack, was executed.

The 2007 bombings in London were caused by homemade organic peroxide-based devices packed into rucksacks. They were followed two weeks later by a series of attempted attacks, which failed to cause injury or damage.

The 7/7 attacks occurred the day after London had won its bid to host the 2012 Olympic Games, which had highlighted the city's multicultural reputation.

According to United States government files, which were consistent with those of the United Kingdom, the four suicide bombers who perpetrated the attack were Hasib Hussain, Mohammad Sidique Khan, Germaine Lindsay, and Shehzad Tanweer. Spokane firmly believed there were others involved that have avoided apprehension since 2005.

Agent Yoder had a very specific agenda when he asked for that file, and after days and nights peering through his jeweler's eyeglass, he found him again. The man on the church steps in New York was also the man on the Capitol steps in Harrisburg and was standing alone in the photograph near the Russell Square tube station in London observing the carnage.

CHAPTER 6

ONE MORE PHOTO

RIGHT AFTER THE Black Friday massacre, Liam Spokane and his support staff met with John Rivero, United States attorney of New York, and Rivero's staff. It was the same type of meeting Spokane had in Harrisburg, same debriefing, same result, with Rivero keeping his resentment to himself.

Six months later, June 18, 2015

The long black Denali, with tinted windows, left the headquarters of the division for counterintelligence before daylight. The driver did not speak and carried on his person a holstered nine-millimeter semiautomatic PPK. His passenger, who sat in the front with him, said very little on their trip to Center City Manhattan. The Washington Monument and the White House, both brightly illuminated in the darkness, could be seen from afar as they left the city. Before noon, they would be going through the congested Holland Tunnel, right on schedule, and after arriving at their destination, the two of them were escorted through a private entrance.

Without any hint of what was going on, Yvette Lewis had traveled to New York City with her armed escort and met with the United States attorney in Downtown Manhattan. Her bodyguard had been ordered by Liam Spokane to accompany her at all times. The purpose of the mission was straightforward. She was to bring back all progress reports and developments from the investigation into the Macy's bombings. She was to bring back every photo taken from the Macy's surveillance cameras on every floor. She was to offer no explanation for this retrieval other than that the investigation is ongoing.

Rivero was annoyed by the brevity of the meeting.

Yvette Lewis was not . . . because her mission was accomplished.

Yoder's mission was also accomplished, almost overnight.

The man was there at Macy's on Black Friday and was depicted in a photo on an elevated alcove overlooking the destruction on the first floor of New York's legendary department store. Others in the photo appeared panic-stricken and running for the exits. The mystery man, however, was calmly standing there, observing. The blowup of color photographs graphically illustrated the blood spatter throughout the marble floors and walls, the bodies, and the desperately injured, which included scores of small children crying.

"We've got to find this motherfucker," Spokane said as he stared at the fourth photo of the man brought to him by Yoder.

Yoder said nothing.

Yvette said nothing.

"Every catastrophe where he appeared had been planned and executed by al-Qaeda or ISIS. The son of a bitch just shows up, does whatever he does, and leaves. I've had agents in the field all over the world since the first match, his presence in Harrisburg in 2015 and at the Twin Towers in 2001. My agents, including that confidential informant toward whom I'm developing increased suspicion, keep coming back empty-handed. Nobody knows who he is in the terrorist world. Nobody has ever seen him or talked to him, and that's bullshit . . . It's not possible," Spokane said as the frustration in his voice mounted.

"Dammit. What's our next move?" Spokane asked, looking directly at Yoder.

Yvette shifted her gaze to Yoder as well.

Yoder took a deep breath and responded quickly, obviously expecting the question.

"I don't know what this man's assignment or role is, but he obviously has no fear. He shows up at these catastrophes and makes no effort to conceal his presence. He did it in 2001 in New York. He did it in 2007 in London. He did it in on Black Friday last year. He did it this year in Harrisburg. He's obviously on the move. He's also somebody

WILLIAM C. COSTOPOULOS

that nobody is going to dime out, and I mean nobody," Yoder said, summarizing his thoughts; however, he was not yet finished.

"We know there will be another act of terrorism. The last two were within one year, and the terrorist world is in proactive mode. We don't know where . . . We don't know when . . . We don't know the target . . . We just know it'll happen. I believe he'll show up, and I think that when it does happen in the near future, we must have boots on the ground with one mission before the smoke clears . . . and that because he'll be there, we'll be able to take him down. I really think it's imperative that we take him alive. He's too important."

CHAPTER 7

THE BIG APPLE

September 9, 2015
United States Attorney's Office
Foley Square
Manhattan, New York

J OHN RIVERO, THE United States attorney for the Southern
District of New York, was overlooking the New York City streets
from his high-rise office on Foley Square. He had his own power base;
the Southern District of New York encompasses the boroughs of
Manhattan and the Bronx, along with Dutchess, Orange, Putnam,
Rockland, Sullivan, and Westchester counties. His office prosecutes
cases involving violations of federal law and represents the interests of the
United States government in criminal and civil matters. The magnitude
of such responsibility is undisputed, for it requires investigation and
prosecution of cases even when the conduct arises in foreign countries.

John Rivero was a proud man, with good reason, for his office was
one of the nation's premier legal institutions, successfully prosecuting
groundbreaking and historic cases. Those who have served in the
Southern District include lawyers who have gone on to become United
States senators, congressmen, mayors of New York City, governor of
New York, secretary of war, secretary of homeland security, secretary
of state, attorney general of the United States, United States Supreme
Court justice, ambassadors, and federal judges.

His army of men and women in the federal courtrooms of New
York were trained and experienced litigators, and in every criminal
term, they would try a wide array of cases—white-collar and cyber

crime, mortgage fraud, public corruption, gang violence, organized crime, international narcotics trafficking, *and terrorism*—and in every criminal term, they would kick ass.

Those high-paid criminal defense lawyers with their fancy silk suits and gold Rolex watches would beg for plea bargains to avoid trying a case because they knew what they were up against.

To Rivero, perception also played a key role in his office and the courtrooms. His army of attorneys was required to look like attorneys who prosecuted cases for the United States government. In the courtrooms, his dress code dictated blue or gray suits accessorized with conservative ties and shoes. If his litigators were not trying a case but working in their offices preparing to do so, blue or gray suits with ties and conservative shoes was also the dress code . . . never blue jeans, casual shirts, or sandals. Even the support staff of secretaries, paralegals, and administrators was to look professional.

That morning, John was alone in his office and had been there from the early morning hours, which was his routine. He was already smoking a cigar, a dark tobacco Rocky Patel Edge, trying to cope with his anger and frustration. That bombing at Macy's, one day after Thanksgiving, one day after the Macy's day parade, was in his backyard. He considered that to be his house, and it was not only an alarm felt in Washington DC, but to him, it was a personal affront.

To add to his stressful complex of emotions was unprecedented annoyance.

That first meeting in his office with the counterterrorist division from Washington DC—Liam Spokane and his entourage—busted his balls. Those fucking guys might be pretty good at investigating cases but no better than his office even at the international level, and they didn't know shit about working up a case for trial.

They must have forgotten that he personally prosecuted the 1993 World Trade Center bombing, one that was a terrorist attack dating back to February 26, 1993, when a truck bomb was detonated below the north tower of the World Trade Center in New York City. The 1,336 pounds (606 kilograms) urea nitrate-hydrogen gas-enhanced device was intended to knock the north tower into the south tower, bringing both towers down and killing tens of thousands of people. It failed to do so but did kill six people and injured more than one thousand.

Rivero's office put that case together and personally tried it. He himself convicted four men for carrying out the bombing—Abouhalima, Ajaj, Ayyad, and Salameh—of terrorism and mass murder. In November 1997, he personally convicted Ramzi Yousef, the mastermind behind the bombings, and Eyad Ismoil, who drove the truck carrying the bomb.

The boys in Washington must have forgotten *that*.

Rivero had been a federal prosecutor for twenty-eight years and became a young assistant prosecutor right out of New York University School of Law. For twenty-eight years, he lived in the courtrooms and was extremely persuasive. He would get the jury's attention in his opening, paint his picture with direct, dismantle the defense with cross, and put it all together in his closing. His presence in the courtroom was commanding, and his portly frame added to his style. His jet-black hair seemed to get thicker over the years and gave him a look of distinction and credibility.

September 9, 2015, 7:45a.m. Down below, Rivero watched the busy streets of Lower Manhattan. People were already walking in both directions on the sidewalk. Everybody was on a cell phone, there were no greetings exchanged, other pedestrians were talking to themselves almost robotically; there seemed to be a human disconnect. Cabs were dropping off and picking up, and transit buses were doing the same. There were very few limousines since his offices were not on Wall Street. Rivero wondered if those people were aware that in two days, the world would be reminded once again of 9/11.

That second visit from the counterterrorism division in Washington also made him crazy. Liam Spokane had sent up that Victoria's Secret model to take his file, and although she was polite enough, it still busted his ass. He had heard nothing from Washington since Black Friday, absolutely nothing, but he wasn't waiting around for them to do his work. He had already investigated and determined that the bombs were activated by a timed device, were sophisticated in nature, and were strategically placed on Thanksgiving night. Six hooded terrorists, with semiautomatic weapons, silencers attached, entered after closing hours, corralled Macy's nighttime security force, threatened them with their lives, and threatened to cut off their children's heads if they said anything before the timed explosions. Their lives were spared to avoid

WILLIAM C. COSTOPOULOS

alerting the authorities before the planned attack, and the security force complied.

No one has been identified to date, but that's how it happened. Washington DC had not known about that, but they would now since Ms. Yvette Lewis picked up the file.

If the demeaning position into which the Washington folks had placed him weren't bad enough, it was exacerbated by that goofy United States attorney in Harrisburg that kept calling him for updates and trying to impress upon him his fucking "lone wolf" theory. Sam Nelson, who liked to be called Samson, and his entire office had obviously spent too much time in Penn's Woods worrying about wolves. Nelson kept telling him about the sequence of events, reminding him about the threat of "Jihadi John" and how "Jihadi John" was going to get us with wolves. That "Jihadi John" was nothing but a fucking nut in a Halloween suit, and Rivero was sick and tired of hearing about him from Nelson.

The silence in Rivero's office and his reflections were broken by his receptionist who had brought in his memos for the day, debriefing him on the status of the important cases in his office.

"Mr. Rivero," she said, handing him his coffee for the morning.

"Yes?"

"Sam Nelson called a few minutes ago wanting to know if you had any updates."

"Did he sound like he was out in the woods?" Rivero snapped sarcastically and lit up another cigar.

CHAPTER 8

PENN'S WOODS

September 9, 2015
United States Attorney's Office
Harrisburg, Pennsylvania

S AMUEL NELSON WAS also irritated and frustrated at how
things were going. The bombing and fire on State Street was the
first act of war by terrorists on Pennsylvania soil, if you did not count
the plane that went down in Somerset County on September 11, 2001.
It was the biggest case in his office. The media was clamoring, calling
him every day for comment, and the boys in Washington weren't telling
him anything.

Even that asshole Rivero in New York wasn't returning his calls.
Nelson was convinced that what happened in Harrisburg was an ISIS
attack by a radicalized American citizen or more than one. That's what
the "lone wolf" assault "Jihadi John" had promised months before
was all about. The devastation brought about on State Street was not
sophisticated. The single bomb that was used consisted of the same
material used in the Oklahoma City bombing on April 19, 1995.

The bombing of the Alfred P. Murrah Federal Building in
Downtown Oklahoma City was a domestic terror attack carried out
by two American citizens, Timothy McVeigh, and Terry Nichols. It
was a bombing that killed 168 people, injured more than 680 others,
destroyed or damaged 324 buildings within a 16-block radius, destroyed
or burned 86 cars, and shattered glass in 258 nearby buildings, causing
at least an estimated $652 million worth of damage.

They may have not called those two terrorists "lone wolves" back in 1995 . . . but that's what they were . . . and they used the same materials for their bomb as the bomb retrieved from State Street. In addition, McVeigh and Nichols were Americans who hated government and law enforcement and who were troubled with mental health issues . . . all of which are characteristics of a "lone wolf" terrorist.

A single "lone wolf," or a pack of them, can strike a site in any big city such as Macy's in New York or a transportation hub. They can strike at a major sporting event like the Boston Marathon. They can strike at war memorials as they did in Canada. They can attack schools and shoot students for revenge. They can attack shopping malls. Even the most unlikely small-town coffee shop could be a target. They can randomly shoot naive civilians or unsuspecting police.

Like the "lone wolf" did in Pike County. It was exactly one year ago, September 12, 2014, one day after the thirteenth anniversary of 9/11, that a "lone wolf" by the name of Eric Matthew Frein ambushed and murdered an innocent Pennsylvania State Police officer who was walking to his car at night preparing to return home to his wife and children. Eric Frein, thirty-one years old, who described himself as a self-taught survivalist and was also a known expert marksman, murdered the trooper sniper style with a .308 high-powered, scope-mounted rifle and seriously wounded another uniformed officer who was also there. It all happened outside the local Pike County state police barracks in the Pocono Mountains during a shift change late at night.

Why?

Because Eric Frein had a grudge against law enforcement personnel; he hated them as he did the American government, and he felt it was time to do something about it. To Samuel Nelson, United States attorney for the Middle District, this "lone wolf" assassination was very, very disconcerting. It happened to be in his district, and Nelson was very much involved in that case.

Nelson's district did not have the population base of Manhattan, but geographically, it encompassed the entirety of Central Pennsylvania. It included Scranton, a hard-working, blue-collar town, rough around the edges, with a history of organized crime and political corruption. It included Williamsport, home of the Little League World Series, which brings in visitors from around the globe every August.

It included Lewisburg, home to Allenwood Federal Prison Camp (the residence of President Nixon's coconspirators) and Lewisburg Federal Penitentiary (the residence of more hardened federal convicts). It included Harrisburg, Pennsylvania's capital city and seat of government and an obvious target for terrorists to choose as settings to carry out their nefarious schemes.

The anguish that Nelson suffered as a result of the killing and serious injuring of those two Pennsylvania State Police officers was exacerbated by how long it took to apprehend this one wolf who had no support or training by the ISIS hierarchy. The police search team increased from two hundred to four hundred and then to a thousand. The manhunt included local police; state police forces from Pennsylvania, New York, and New Jersey; the FBI; the United States Marshals Service; and the Bureau of Alcohol, Tobacco, and Firearms. Tracking dogs were used but were thrown off the trail when Frein successfully evaded them on foot by using water crossings and taking advantage of terrain conditions.

Equipment used in the search included numerous police vehicles, armored BearCats, at least four helicopters with thermal-imaging equipment, and a thirteen-thousand-pound, $245,000, Ring Power–armored siege vehicle dubbed "The Rook." The FBI displayed Frein's image and the number of a state police hotline on hundreds of digital billboards in Pennsylvania and five other states that are controlled by Outdoor Advertising Association of America.

Police believed they had seen Frein several times during their search but each time were unable to approach directly due to the rugged terrain of the area, which allowed Frein to slip away. The state police believed Frein was taunting them, and Lt. Col. George Bivens told reporters, "I almost think this is a game to him." The difficulty of capturing Frein was compared to that of finding other survivalist outdoorsmen such as Eric Rudolph, Troy James Knapp, Jason McVean, and Robert William Fisher, all of whom were able to elude police for years with their special training.

Frein was finally captured by United States marshals, *Nelson's people*, on October 30, 2014, forty-eight days after the shooting. He was apprehended in an open meadow near an unused airport hangar at Birchwood-Pocono Airport. It was an abandoned airfield, approximately three miles outside of Tannersville, Pennsylvania, not far from the crime scene. At the time of Frein's arrest, which took place without incident, he was unarmed, but a .308 caliber rifle and pistol were recovered. He was restrained using the handcuffs of the murdered officer.

To Samuel Nelson, that massive manhunt was unsettling. It took almost seven weeks, thousands of law enforcement personnel, and millions of dollars in manpower and equipment to capture one asshole. What would we do if more of those "lone wolves" were cut loose?

To Nelson, the terrorist world had unleashed a lone wolf or a pack of them on to Harrisburg.

And Harrisburg was the perfect carcass, for it was the capital city of Pennsylvania and the Commonwealth's seat of state government and law enforcement. It was an easy target. The entire city had a population base of less than fifty thousand, and much of the population lived in poverty. Ironically, one of its most famous cultural events, begun in 1917 and held annually in mid-January, is the Pennsylvania Farm Show. No wonder it was a feeding ground for wolves.

The Pennsylvania State Capitol is the cornerstone of Harrisburg and is home to the Commonwealth of Pennsylvania's legislature. It was designed in 1902 in a Beaux-Arts style with Renaissance themes throughout. It is a magnificent architectural monument, and it looks very much like the United States Capitol in Washington DC. Pennsylvania's Capitol houses the chambers for the Pennsylvania General Assembly made up of the House of Representatives and the Senate and the Harrisburg chambers for the supreme and superior courts of Pennsylvania, as well as the offices of the governor and lieutenant governor.

To Samuel Nelson, the bombing and torching of State Street at the foot of the Capitol was not a coincidence. The tracks were those of a wolf, a wolf who hated government and law enforcement. Those carnivorous animals, with or without mental health issues, seemed to be more prevalent today than ever before. The McVeighs and Freins of the world were right here in America; no passports needed. The radicalization of these disgruntled misfits was an easy task for ISIS, and it was frustrating and frightening to the United States attorney for the Middle District. He had recently heard in the news that even young women from Chicago were using their own money to fly to terrorist countries to join the cause.

His first trial assistant, Fran Korsakov, was a good listener and would never challenge his boss. While he wasn't completely convinced that the "lone wolf" theory made sense, he also wasn't totally free of suspicion that it might actually have some credence.

CHAPTER 9

MOSCOW

October 16, 2015
Sheremetyevo International Airport
Moscow, Russia

A MAJESTIC SUNSET was on the horizon, and darkness would soon fall upon the vast Sheremetyevo International Airport, northwest of Central Moscow. The airport was a hub for passenger operations of the Russian international airline Aeroflot and was one of three major airports that serve Moscow. Major airlines, most notably Lufthansa, British Airways, Iberia, Japan Airlines, Brussels Airlines, Austrian Airlines, and Swiss International, were arriving and departing throughout the day and night with all commands coming from air traffic control. Thousands of passengers from every country would go through exhaustive security checks before boarding, while those arriving would go through customs. Some individuals who fit certain profiles would be taken aside for cavity searches.

On the departure end of this active runway, devoid of any other flights, sat a lone aircraft. All others had been held at their respective gates by ground controllers. The Airbus was scheduled to depart Moscow at 7:30 p.m. Russian time. Because of the eight-hour difference in New York and the estimated eleven hours of flight time, the scheduled arrival time at JFK International Airport was 10:30 p.m. EST. This was no ordinary aircraft, and this was no ordinary passenger list.

The aircraft was a 300 series Airbus, which normally carried over 150 passengers with first-class accommodations. This particular plane, however, had been reconfigured, designed, and built to carry sixty with no compromise of floor space. Every swivel seat on the plane was leather, could be converted to a single bed, and was equipped with a personal flat screen TV and other acoustic luxuries. It included two private suites with queen-size beds in each and carried fifteen thousand gallons of water for leisurely showers. The fuel capacity could carry that plane from Moscow to anywhere in the world nonstop. This Airbus was made in Toulouse, France, custom designed with specifications directly from Russia's oligarchy.

And it was Russia's oligarchs who were making this trip to America. Those making the flight were thirty-two of Russia's richest financiers and businessmen, with most of their wealth having come from oil and the global financial market. The additional twenty-two passengers were wives and girlfriends, as well as the highest-paid and most beautiful Russian hookers.

The purpose of the trip was a scheduled business conference in Manhattan, New York, to be attended on America's end by the CEOs of Goldman Sachs, Bank of America, Morgan Stanley, JP Morgan, and the leading oil barons of the Free World. This meeting would determine global interest rates worldwide and the cost and availability of oil in every country and depending on decisions made would determine how much richer everyone present would be when the conference was over.

This business conference had been planned for over a year and was scheduled to last for three days. Not even the acrimony between this country under the Obama administration and President Putin would interfere. Neither the invasion of Ukraine by Russia nor the downed Malaysian plane that took hundreds of innocent lives in Ukrainian skies on July 17, 2014, nor the controversy and finger-pointing surrounding that terrorist act would interfere with this historic meeting.

After all, business is business at this level.

The scheduled conference was to take place at the prestigious Plaza Hotel, Central Park South, and Fifth Avenue. Two floors had been rented by the affluent Russians. It didn't matter that one suite cost $5,900 a night, since money was no object. In addition to the important business to be conducted, this contingent was planning on having a good time because Russians believe you cannot make good business decisions when you are stressed out or sober. Because planning and timing are everything, the 300 series Airbus was stocked with the finest vodka and scotch, all vintage. The receiving committee in America awaiting the late arrival understood the agenda perfectly.

All flight plans were registered in Moscow and in New York.

The cockpit would be manned by four of Russia's most vetted and experienced pilots, two captains and two first officers.

Though first-class accommodations standards suggest one airline flight attendant per twenty passengers, this privileged group would have four, all vetted, all multilingual, all beautiful and scantily clad, with instructions that no passenger's needs were to be unattended. The job description for the flight attendants was understood and agreed to, and they would be paid well . . . This was not union work.

This Airbus was the ultimate party bus, and it departed the Sheremetyevo International Airport precisely as scheduled, 7:30 p.m. Russian time.

Within an hour of being airborne, the vodka, Chivas Regal, and champagne all were flowing freely. The shashlik was prepared to order; there was lobster and fresh fish on demand and all-you-can-eat caviar. Two of the airline stewardesses already were unavailable for serving food but were earning their salaries in the two suites. At one time while they were missing, six male passengers were out of their assigned seats. With the two suites occupied, the hookers were servicing the Russian men in plain view without shame, making some wives uncomfortable and some not and others envious.

It seemed that no one was interested in getting a good night's sleep, and with the frequent outbursts of laughter and cheer, it would have been impossible anyway. The flight itself was very smooth. There was no turbulence, the night was clear, all systems were "go," and unlike the airline stewardesses, the team in the cockpit was all business. Indeed, the door to their flight compartment was securely locked, and instructions were that they were not to be interrupted.

At approximately 10:00 p.m. Eastern time, all four personnel in the cockpit could see the magnificent skyline of New York during their approach to land from thirty miles away. Manhattan looked very much awake with its brightly lit high-rises and rivers and thoroughfares in the distance. It was time for them to begin their slow but gradual descent onto the active runway at JFK, and based on their current approach at ten thousand feet, the landing would be right on schedule.

Air traffic control at JFK gave the 300 series Airbus clearance to land.

The two captains at the controls simultaneously felt that something suddenly had gone drastically wrong mechanically. The landing gear did not engage, and they were not descending at a normal rate or degree expected for an aircraft of this size. In fact, the pilots had no control over the flight management system from this moment on.

At air traffic control, the radar indicated that the Airbus from Moscow was losing altitude too rapidly and radioed the aircraft to correct its position immediately.

"We are experiencing serious mechanical difficulty," the first captain answered. His answer was controlled, but the anxiety in his voice was undeniable.

"Then you must deviate immediately" came the response from the tower. "Head southwest, fly heading 240 degrees to assess problem, and advise your intentions."

There was no response from the Airbus.

"I said you must deviate immediately!" The command was given again, this time with urgency.

And for the second time, there was no response from the Airbus. Within minutes, the personnel at air traffic control could see the suspect plane overshoot JFK, and as soon as that happened, and when no response was received, they called for military jets to take to the sky. Almost instantaneously, the drastic request was put into motion. As though the fighter jets were waiting for the call, they were airborne with the most awful of military assignments . . . to destroy that aircraft in flight in order to minimize the loss of human life on the ground.

But even they were too late with their quick response, for within minutes of overshooting JFK, the 300 series Airbus from Moscow plunged into a wooded, unoccupied area, the New Jersey Pine Barrens. The explosion on impact could be seen and heard for endless miles, and no one would survive that crash.

* * *

At 10:35 p.m., the emergency alert went directly to Liam Spokane.

The terrorist attack that his office knew was coming had just occurred.

WILLIAM C. COSTOPOULOS

There were no details provided other than when and where.

By 11:15 p.m., with the fire still raging, and though there were already emergency personnel at the scene, Liam Spokane had his men on the ground, fifty of them . . . all armed, all with night vision binoculars, all with one assignment. That assignment was to see if the man in the photos would appear.

They would not be disappointed.

He was standing on a hill watching the fire burn . . . alone . . . just watching.

He was surrounded by Spokane's army . . . all had their AK-47s drawn . . . but the official reports of that take-down were all consistent. The man on the hill offered no resistance . . . made no effort to get away . . . and said nothing when he was approached and handcuffed.

CHAPTER 10

QUICK RESPONSES

October 17, 2015

A T 6:15 A.M., the rescue and investigative teams were making very little progress at the crash site in the Jersey Pine Barrens because the Russian Airbus was still aflame. Black smoke billowed in the early morning sky in stark contrast to the blue horizon, sending another visual image of fear and terror throughout Manhattan.

Televised throughout the world, camera crews and commentators converged, microphones in hand, from every major network—ABC, CBS, NBC, CNN, Fox, and BBC—adding fuel to the frenzy and panic. The backdrop of fire and smoke, engines and sirens, the tail of the plane still identifiable in the wreckage with its Russian emblem was right out of a war movie.

Human bodies had been ejected from the plane on impact. Cameras filmed the cadavers being moved, placed in body bags, and loaded on to motortrucks by rescue teams. The retrieval process was done carefully and with respect, and there was no looting. All personal items—jewelry, cell phones, laptops, remnants of wallets and photos, passports, and cash—were inventoried and put into glassine bags. The identification of those bodies, and return of personal items, would be left to the Russian authorities once the deceased were flown back to their home country.

Fire truck hoses continued to stream water onto the fuselage, but the search for anyone living was futile. Everyone on that aircraft was killed on impact, fifty-four passengers, four cockpit crew members, four airline stewardesses; only the cockpit crew members were still in the aircraft, strapped securely to their seats, locked in their chamber of death.

Because of the intense heat and smoke, the Federal Aviation Administration (FAA) would be hampered in the retrieval of the black box and electronic data to determine the cause. The communications between air traffic control and the captains were all intact as were all radar graphics memorializing the missile's flight and rapid descent. Theories of what happened were rampant, pundits on the major networks who were former pilots opined that either it was an interior job in the cockpit by a rogue pilot or the plane had been hotwired in a manner to render the pilots helpless and put the aircraft on autopilot to its point of impact.

In Russia, within hours of notification that *their* Airbus had crashed and burned, their investigative team searched the homes of the pilots, of the airline stewardesses, and of every passenger on board. They were not fooling around and doing what had to be done, but President Putin and his closest advisors did not believe that one of their own was responsible. Putin and his boys had their own theories. The United States was not ruled out as a suspect nor was Ukraine, al-Qaeda, or ISIS.

The apologetic call and expressed sympathy from President Obama to President Putin was accepted with caution and would be part of Obama's worldwide speech that night. Obama also invited Putin to send his investigative teams to America to participate in the investigation of this tragedy, an invitation Putin accepted. Within one hour of that call, he had a private jet of Russian crash site investigators on their way.

Manhattan and all of America was put on red alert. The alert system was color-coded, and red is as serious as it gets. All major transit systems in Manhattan were shut down, bridges were off-limits until further notice, businesses were closed by order of the governor, and because it was a Saturday, Wall Street was quiet.

* * *

If the breaking news of another 9/11 act of terrorism on American soil was not enough, another break in the nonstop news cycle occurred at 7:45 a.m., perfectly timed, when a published video from ISIS hit the airwaves. The message was to let the world know that ISIS was claiming responsibility and impressing upon the world the Islamic State of Iraq's and Syria's capability and reach. This Islamic act of hate and destruction was an example of more to come.

This newly released video depicted five Islamic terrorists sitting at a table, all hooded in black, with one in the middle acting as spokesman. He was flanked by two others on each side, all four of them holding menacing semiautomatic rifles with fifty-round clips, and bandoliers of rounds draped across their bodies.

"Good morning," the spokesman eerily began. "We have very long memories, and we do not forgive. Fifty of our brothers and sisters were murdered by the Russians in 2002 in Moscow. It was April 23, 2002. Surely, Mr. Putin remembers when his dogs pumped gas and chemicals into the Dubrovka Theater causing instant sickness and death to our loved ones. Movsar Barayev was one of them . . . He was my father."

"Our only regret," the spokesman continued in his threatening voice, "is that the plane missed our intended American demons in Manhattan. We will not miss in the future.

"Have a good day."

Just like that, the video went blank, the message taking less than twenty seconds.

Whoever was not awake at that hour throughout the world for this premier showing would have the clip presented to them over and over for weeks to come, with frequent splices on the screen depicting the nightmare scene in the Pine Barrens. The only caveat from the major networks was a brief message for parents to spare their children the graphic footage and audio.

Pres. Barack Obama was very much awake at 7:45 a.m., as he had been throughout the night, and watched the breaking news from ISIS while sitting behind his desk in the Oval Office in Washington DC. He was accompanied by Liam Spokane, his hand-picked, trusted director of counterintelligence and his most recently appointed secretary of defense. Liam Spokane had debriefed the president with his intelligence gathering, which included every detail about "the man" captured at the crash site, a person of great interest, who had been taken to an undisclosed location.

The president watched the ISIS video in silence.

So did Liam Spokane.

So did the secretary of defense, who believed an immediate military response had to be made and was hoping for presidential authorization.

Without coaxing, President Obama knew and understood that his strategy to degrade and ultimately destroy ISIS wasn't working. He had promised the American people to keep their sons out of harm's way, that there would be no "boots on the ground." It was a promise he believed the American people embraced, but *something* had to be done. That *something* was not an easy call because the enemy here was elusive and difficult to identify, always surrounding themselves with innocent people and children, their identities hidden under black hoods. Yet the president knew by 8:00 p.m. that the nation and the entire world were awaiting America's response.

Before his meeting with Spokane and his secretary of defense ended that morning, the president ordered daily updates on "the man" in custody. No one in that room knew or had any idea who he was, but all were convinced that he was a major player of indescribable evil. Nevertheless, the president made it clear to Spokane that though the interrogations of their suspect could be intense and protracted, it was not to include torture such as waterboarding, and this presidential order was not to be violated.

"Understood?" the president asked looking directly at Spokane.

Spokane nodded affirmatively but actually did not understand. Liam Spokane's history was not in the cloistered world of the White House, with its magnificent decor, chandeliers, and antique treasures. His world was not on the elegant floor of Congress, adorned with mahogany, oriental rugs, and stained glass, with only microphones as weaponry. Spokane's world was in the streets and caves of Iraq, Iran, Pakistan, and Syria, where even a child of tender years could carry knapsacks filled with timed devices to kill American soldiers and their allies.

America's use of torture and waterboarding in the past did not compare to the interrogation methods of the enemy, which included amputation of fingers, hands, ears, and now heads. Quick and reliable information sometimes requires coercion, and history has borne out that it works, even American style. The president, even if he understood that reality, made it clear that civility was America's signature, and as long as he was president of the United States that rule would not change.

Liam Spokane was well aware of the Senate Intelligence Committee's torture report that was released before Christmas in 2014, exposing American hostages and agents to immediate death in retaliation. The report was a scathing criticism of the methods used by CIA agents to extract information from al-Qaeda terrorists who were being held in

Guantanamo Bay, Cuba, immediately after 9/11. Among the detainees was Abu Hudhayfa, who was "subjected to ice water baths and sixty-six hours of standing sleep deprivation" before the CIA discovered that he was probably "not the person he was believed to be." Other coercive measures set forth in the report included waterboarding, which is torture by simulating drowning, and Khalid Sheikh Mohammed was identified as a prisoner who was waterboarded 183 times. If waterboarding did not bring about the desired information, the prisoner would be placed in a coffin-size confinement box for ten days at a time.

Spokane was well aware of all that. He was also aware that the CIA responded to that report, affirming that torture works when information is critical and time is of the essence, that these measures saved the lives of American citizenry and may have thwarted a nuclear attack on Manhattan.

"Understood?" the president asked Spokane again, not satisfied that Spokane just shook his head. "I know how you feel about my position on this matter, and that you're unhappy with my support of the report's conclusions and release. But even though we're in the midst of volatile times in the world, the civility of America must not be compromised."

"I understand, Mr. President," Spokane answered.

"One final presidential order," President Obama added. "This recent capture was a remarkable piece of work. The suspect is not to be treated as a prisoner of war. Such a designation will simply mean that he'll languish in Guantanamo at government expense. I don't know who he is, but I believe he's important, and we risk the terrorist world rallying behind him, creating a new messiah. He is to be indicted, tried, and convicted in our courts and in the world court of public opinion. After that, I don't care if he's put to death."

* * *

8:00 p.m. Eastern time
East room of White House, Washington DC

President Barack Obama stood with both hands on the podium adorned with the round seal identifying that he was the president of the United States. To his right stood the Republican speaker of the House and to his left the Republican Senate majority leader.

Liam Spokane was already gone and, as the president spoke, was at the undisclosed location, peering through a one-way window, watching an interrogation of "the man" that was under way. This interrogation was to be done by Spokane's top interrogator, with the detainee shackled and handcuffed, the handcuffs locked onto the interrogation table. The viewing audience would include George Yoder, Yvette Lewis, a psychiatrist, interpreters, other experienced interrogators in counterintelligence, and the Muslim confidential informant.

The president's audience was not so limited, and they were not looking through a one-way glass. The media had been waiting for hours, and the cameras began rolling as the president walked to the podium, his entourage already in place. His audience was the American people, but all those in the Free World, Russia, and beyond were listening.

President Obama's speechwriters had spent all day carefully wording what was to be said. It was a daunting task. On September 10, 2014, they wrote one speech when the American journalists were beheaded, a speech emphasizing that America would degrade and destroy ISIS. One day after Black Friday, November 28, 2014, they wrote another speech when Macy's was bombed, a speech announcing that America was ramping up its operations. They wrote a third speech after Harrisburg, Pennsylvania, suffered its terrorist attack on State Street, a speech pointing out that Pennsylvania's Capitol and Federal Buildings, the intended targets, had escaped being bombed because of the precautions in place. Now the speechwriters were dealing with the crash of a Russian jet plane that had crashed and burned on American soil minutes from Manhattan, killing everybody on board and still burning as they composed it. It was a difficult speech to write.

President Obama maintained his calm for the sake of the nation. His articulate style was desperately needed by his audience, and politics at this hour would have to be set aside by both parties. This was an easy sell when Obama called the leaders of the House and Senate earlier that day. He had been having a bad year having lost the Senate in the last election and was now burdened with a Republican House majority and the ongoing clamor over Obamacare. Yet he knew, and his supporters and detractors knew, that America needed him to respond as commander in chief of the armed forces.

THE WHITE HOUSE: "My fellow Americans, tonight I want to speak to you about the tragedy that has brought great sorrow to the entire free world. A Russian aircraft filled with innocent citizens of that country crashed less than twenty-four hours ago in the Pine Barrens of New Jersey. It brings me no comfort that the intended target of this barbarism was Russia and not the United States, although the plane fell on our soil.

I have already called President Putin to express America's grief over this tragedy. Although Mr. Putin and I have our differences, in this moment, we are friends and allies, and together, we will seek out this ruthless organization known as ISIS and bring them to justice. For the first time, America and Russia have created a formal alliance against terrorism. I welcome their support: their investigators are already at the crime scene, and I personally intend to meet with President Putin in Russia within ten days to solidify this alliance. Our tactics and strategies may be separate and apart in format but not in resources or commitment. For me to define our respective roles right now is premature, but this country can be assured that progress is being made so our children may inherit a life of liberty and the pursuit of happiness, which is the basis for all that is American."

The media correspondents and reporters were interrupting each other to get their questions out. What's the new strategy? Do you agree the old strategy isn't working? Are you going to put boots on the ground? Are you simply going to ignore the Malaysian flight that was blown out of the sky over Ukraine? What if Russia continues to invade Ukraine? Has the claim by ISIS been confirmed by the United States? By Russia?

Ah, but President Obama, the ultimate presenter when it comes to hard answers, kept going back to his theme: that this alliance with Russia to combat terrorism was formidable, and while it didn't mean they were going to be friends forever on all other issues, that now terrorists of the world would have to deal with the two most powerful countries on

WILLIAM C. COSTOPOULOS

earth, both now pledged to a mission of destruction for these extremists. America and Russia may be coming from opposite directions, but they would meet in the middle with a resounding crescendo.

"May God bless our troops, may God bless the United States of America, and may God bless Russia."

Under the circumstances, he had pulled it off exceptionally well.

* * *

The Russian spy network—for intelligence and counterintelligence gathering—is recognized as one of the most effective in the world. Scotland Yard in London is second contender for that title and the United States a distant third.

The reason?

In Russia, the cloak-and-dagger men and women in the field of espionage are groomed, educated, and trained from childhood on. Their methods of surveillance and obtaining information are sophisticated, technologically advanced, surreptitious, and aggressive when the need arises.

It is suspected they walk the halls of the Pentagon.

The streets of London.

The shrines of the Far East.

One reason Russian spies are very good at what they do relates directly to their total lack of restrictions and limitations . . . There are simply none at all. They have no interest or regard for civil liberties or constitutional safeguards, such as due process. Civility is for other countries that need to foster and protect an image worldwide. For them, civility hampers and interferes with getting needed information, and such interference makes it difficult to obtain justice (at least justice as they see it).

President Putin was at one time a member of the KGB, the Soviet intelligence agency, and a firm believer in information gathering by whatever means, for without information, you can't be intelligent. This downed plane, which took the lives of Russian innocents, rallied much-needed global support for his country . . . and for him personally.

Within seventy-two hours of the downed Airbus incident, and within sixty-three hours of the ISIS video announcement claiming responsibility, a contingent of Russian soldiers had taken over a military stronghold in the mountains of Northern Afghanistan controlled by ISIS radicals. The small band of Russian soldiers stormed a fortified house and after a brief exchange of gunfire made a forced entry, lined up five Islamist militants against the wall, and executed them at point-blank range, one at a time. They were not questioned prior to the execution. They had no rights read to them, no grand jury, and no trial; they were simply lined up and shot.

They were the same five who claimed responsibility on TV. The Russian spy network had "found them out" when they were tipped off by an al-Qaeda soldier who was one of their own confidential informants in the field. The al-Qaeda organization was irate that ISIS claimed responsibility, knowing that the downing of the Airbus was not actually their doing. ISIS is a spin-off of al-Qaeda, and to scoop al-Qaeda publicly and possibly without basis was not considered an acceptable terrorist tactic.

President Putin forwarded the color photos of the bloody scene to President Obama with graphic shots of each ISIS terrorist riddled with bullet holes lying on the ground. It included a panoramic view of all five dead together, along with a photo of the four semiautomatic rifles propped up against the wall and a final one of five black hoods and black outer robes hanging in a closet.

Mission accomplished by Russia.

No press conferences were scheduled.

CHAPTER 11

INTERROGATIONS

F ROM THE MOMENT "the person of interest" was captured on the hill, he was put on his knees, handcuffed behind his back, and shackled and blindfolded before being shoved into an armored transport vehicle to be taken to his new home. In less than three hours, the prisoner had all restraints removed, was processed, and then placed in a ten-square-foot padded cell with no windows. No one had asked him any questions in transit, and he had not offered to speak.

Before the lockup, he was strip-searched. Every cavity in his body was penetrated for the reason that timed explosives can be placed anywhere if you're willing to die in the process. The inventory of his belongings produced very little: no wallet, no passport, no identification whatsoever, no jewelry, some cash, but no negotiable instruments of trade.

The man was being held at an undisclosed location near CIA Headquarters, Washington DC. The site was a maximum security facility designed to withstand an attack, staffed by perimeter guards, and equipped with electronic surveillance cameras. This was not a detention facility for street criminals but was designed for absolute confinement. There were multiple interrogation rooms, all with one-way observation windows, concealed video cameras, high-tech audio recorders, and restraining devices at the interrogation tables. Escape was impossible.

Some of the rooms for questioning were starker than others—steel tables anchored to the floor, two chairs, barren walls—while others were more comfortable, with upholstered furniture for lounging and coffee tables. The room assigned for questioning would be determined after assessing the inmate's security risk, willingness to talk, and measures designed to encourage dialogue. They were all set up, however, for immediate intervention by outside help if the subject being interrogated created a threat.

On paper, he was being detained as a material witness pursuant to 18 U.S. C.A. 3144, a statute that allows the federal government to hold an important witness who is a flight risk. In fact, the strategy was to get as much information from him as possible using sleep deprivation, psychological terror, and the unknown of possible torture. The plan was then to prosecute him for mass murder and terrorism and, after affording him a trial by jury and due process, to put him to death by lethal injection. Actually, he was no material witness. He was a mastermind of death who was going to meet his maker.

Death by injection was the end game.

Getting him to talk was quite another matter.

The effort to determine his identity through forensics turned out to be a failure. His fingerprints were put into the world data bank for comparison but came up "no match." Blood taken for a DNA comparison also yielded the same result. Dental impressions were taken but came up "no match" as well. Hair samples, taken as a matter of routine, were also a worthless exercise. His photograph had already been run on the computer network by Yvette Lewis and circulated by CIA field agents and confidential informants, all to no avail.

It was 7:30 p.m. Eastern time, less than twenty-four hours since the 300 series Airbus had crashed and killed all passengers and thirty minutes before President Obama's speech to the nation and the world. The stark interrogation room was ready; the light was on, the electronics of video and audio were checked, and the viewers were ready to observe through one-way windows. The viewing audience were all classified personnel and sworn to secrecy. They had been selected by Liam Spokane who was in charge and included Agent George Yoder; Agent Yvette Lewis; a psychiatrist authorized to administer truth serum and medications; an expert profiler from Quantico, Virginia; a backup interviewer trained in torture and duress techniques; and Spokane himself.

The subject was brought into the room by two armed personnel. He was still handcuffed and shackled, now dressed in an orange jumpsuit, and while under that level of supervision and control had his hands cuffed to the interview table. He was then left alone for several minutes so the observers could assess his demeanor, which was judged unanimously by everyone as a "no read." The subject just sat there, waiting quietly.

The observers were looking for the subtlest clue to this man's persona. They observed his hands, but there were no observable nervous movements. His feet were planted firmly on the floor. His breathing was light and regular. If kinesics is a science, this man defied all that discipline's studies, and if the eyes of a man are the window to his soul, this man didn't appear to have one.

The interrogator assigned by Liam Spokane was Thomas Cody, aged forty-seven, who was highly skilled at his job. A mesomorph of medium height, he was clean-shaven and sported a military crew cut, and his chiseled face was hardened from years of needing to come across as unfeeling and cold. He could be gentle with his questioning or not. His very persona was threatening; it showed in his piercing dark brown eyes and monotonous voice. From the moment he walked into the room with no pencil or pad, white shirt open at the collar, and standard blue jacket, the audience knew he meant business. Yet when Cody entered, the subject's expressionless face gave no clue as to whether or not he was in any way affected.

Cody pulled up his steel chair across from the subject, crowding his guest, and sat silent for a moment before asking politely, "What is your name, sir?" The man did not answer; he just sat there looking serenely at the examiner. The audience already felt the tension. So did Cody, but he gave no clue.

"Do you know why you are here?" Cody asked.

The man did not answer.

"Then I'll tell you why, sir," said Cody and with that reached into his jacket and pulled out an envelope containing color photographs. He tried to minimize the drama, but everyone knew what was coming . . . except maybe the suspect.

"This first photograph I'm showing you is one of you standing on the steps of a Greek church watching the Twin Towers burn on September 11, 2001," Cody explained, carefully sliding the picture over to the detainee. "Do you agree that's you?"

The man nodded yes one time but did not speak a word.

"This next photograph shows you standing at the subway in London on July 7, 2007, watching the aftermath of the London Transit bombings by four British Islamic jihadists," Cody said, carefully sliding a second print across the table. "Do you agree that's you?"

Again, the man nodded his agreement, showing no surprise or emotion.

"Now in this one, you're standing in an alcove overlooking the first floor of Macy's on Black Friday 2014, watching mass murder and mayhem brought about by four timed bombs," Cody said, showing a third photo to the subject. "Do you agree that's you?" This time, Cody watched intently for a reaction other than a slight movement of the head but got nothing but the same affirmative nod.

"And here you are standing at the top of the Capitol Building steps watching the State Street fire. This photo was taken by a drone at 1:30 a.m. on February 9, 2015. Again, sir, do you agree that's you?" Cody asked, a trace of annoyance in his voice.

The man responded as he had before and continued to sit there, poker-faced.

Cody was running out of patience and pictures. He had, however, one more arrow in his quiver, the group of photos taken within the past twenty-four hours in New Heights, New Jersey. He had lots of them.

"You again?" he asked, abbreviating the question, presenting a fifth and final image, anticipating the response. Again, this one depicted the suspect standing on a hill watching the Russian aircraft burn to oblivion. The picture showed him watching the catastrophe impassively from a position close enough to be within earshot of the explosion and fire from the plane's impact.

The man just sat there, unresponsive.

"Aren't you going to nod your head?" Cody asked sarcastically, but the man remained silent and motionless.

Cody had been in this situation before. He could read these fucking psychopaths like a book. But what he was reading this time was a little different, for this subject appeared to have ice water in his veins. He showed no fear, and there was something eerie about that unruffled demeanor of his as if he were the one in charge. The son of a bitch was handcuffed and shackled, destined to live in a concrete vault until his execution . . . and yet he seemed in control. Maybe because he didn't fear death, a common phenomenon, or torture, a reaction less common. Could he be a psychopath who felt no guilt about his mission, or was he dedicated to some cause in which he believed the ends justify the means? Cody was puzzled but had not given up hope that he could figure this motherfucker out.

Questioning was to continue for twenty-six consecutive days. The team of interrogators would take turns creating days of sleep deprivation for the subject. They would try kindness and threats, but without authorization, many of those threats were nothing more than hollow posturing. Kindness was demonstrated by tone of voice and offers of coffee and pastries. None of it was either accepted by the subject or spurned or rewarded with even one spoken word. At the end, their interrogation produced no name or identity, no motive or explanation, only confirmation that the photos were of him . . . which they already knew.

* * *

The relentless interrogation had spanned almost a month, and although the audience behind the looking glass changed, three people who were constants in the investigation were also suffering sleep deprivation in order to keep pace: Liam Spokane, Agent George Yoder, and Agent Yvette Lewis. Early on, they all agreed that this guy wasn't going to talk. They could continue to keep him as a material witness if necessary because such detention under the act was allowed "to prevent a failure of justice." Keeping him, however, was going to require filing paperwork before the courts. This was an easy task but a waste of time for two reasons: first, he wasn't going to talk no matter how long they kept him, and second, no one had a doubt that he was much more than just a material witness; in fact, he was a major player, if not a mastermind, in the world of terrorism.

The next move was to go to the United States attorney general with the file on this individual, to have him indicted and prosecuted in a court of law, and to put him to death. At least that would make it appear as though the antiterror division of the United States was making some progress and for sure would save the government some money in the long run. The unknowns about him would pale in the face of what they had on him.

"You agree?" Spokane asked Agents Yoder and Lewis after the last interview. The three of them were exhausted as they sat around the coffee table in the area contiguous to the now dark interrogation room.

Agent Yoder stated his affirmative answer quickly, but Agent Lewis initially hesitated and seemed reluctant to weigh in. Finally, she disclosed what had been on her mind for the past several weeks.

"I want to talk to him," she said and continued while Spokane and Yoder, incredulous, stared at her in surprise. "Look, we've got nothing to lose. I'm not delusional, but here's the truth of the matter: there's something very intriguing about this guy, and I just want to talk to him for my own satisfaction. I don't think he'll tell me anything, but I think he'll at least talk to me. Please?"

Her request was granted by Spokane—and Yoder agreed—since there was nothing to lose. Spokane insisted that the stark interrogation room be used, with maximum security behind the steel door. She was instructed not to do anything risky; the subject may be intriguing to her, but he was still a killer.

The drill for the subject was the same.

The room was the same.

The two armed guards who cuffed him to the steel table waited outside the steel door.

And then the changeup came.

Yvette Lewis was now on stage, sitting across from him, with her audience watching intently behind the looking glass. Everybody, including Yvette, noted that he smiled when she walked in. Her demeanor was casual and upbeat. Her sexuality had opened many doors throughout her career, and she knew how and when to use it to her best advantage.

The first thing she did was speak to those assembled behind the looking glass and asked that the handcuffs be removed. The man heard both her request and Spokane's irate negative response through the speaker system. Yvette showed no disappointment or surprise and sat down across from her subject.

"Sir," Yvette began, "My name doesn't matter nor does my reason for being here. I do work for the United States government, and you know that. Furthermore, I have no expectation that you're going to tell me anything. I just wanted to talk to you because I've been watching you from behind that glass for a month, and the fact is that I find you

WILLIAM C. COSTOPOULOS

fascinating. For that reason, I asked to talk to you, and my request was granted. I'm not even a profiler for the government. That's all I can tell you."

The man listened with interest, and everyone could tell that he seemed to relish the distraction . . . but he said nothing.

"If you want me to leave now, I will," she said. "Do you want me to leave?" There was a pause, and then he answered, "Not yet."

Yvette's pleased reaction to her small success was evident. Even the audience appreciated that moment of victory. Yvette wasn't quite sure what her next move was because she hadn't expected him to answer. Yet she was a pro and knew the ball had landed in her court, and she wanted to keep playing; however, that desire would be short-lived.

"Is there anything you want to say to me or ask me?" she asked carefully.

The detainee silently signaled that he did.

"What then?" she asked.

The man answered with a question as though he were a distant uncle. "How's little Jimmy?"

Yvette stiffened herself to avoid detection, but she had become totally unnerved. Everybody behind the glass was also shocked that this mass killer, this world terrorist, knew she had a five-year-old son at home. With forced civility, Yvette thanked "the man" for letting her talk with him and got the hell out of there.

CHAPTER 12

DECISIONS

THE NEXT MOVE was made, and consistent with the president's wishes, Liam Spokane took the file on the detainee personally to the United States attorney general. Her name was Katherine Allen Johnson, appointed by President Obama in January 2015 shortly after Eric Holder, his previous appointee, had resigned. Katherine Johnson had been the sitting United States attorney in Pittsburgh and was the second woman in our nation's history to hold that esteemed office. She was sworn in by Vice President Joe Biden after a fairly easy confirmation by the Senate. The reason she had been chosen from an extensive list of candidates was because of her philosophic allegiance to the president, in the same way she had been loyal to Pres. Bill Clinton who had appointed her to the Western District of Pennsylvania.

She belied her age of sixty, was a 1981 graduate of Duquesne University School of Law, had never been married, and was a career prosecutor. Her long blond hair was not age appropriate, but she was trim and fit, was a marathon runner, and dressed impeccably in business suits. She obviously knew her role in the criminal justice system and understood politics and the importance of dealing with the media and public opinion.

This prearranged meeting with Spokane took place in her conference room, and he was asked to come alone. When he arrived, Attorney General Johnson was already seated at the head of the table. Eight of her staff were in attendance, and they included her most senior lawyers and trusted FBI agents.

United States attorneys conduct trial work in cases where the United States is a party. Those who commit acts of terrorism and mass murder anywhere in America, or elsewhere if the conspiracy originated here, will be dealing with that office, and in all such cases, there would be hell to pay. Referred to as the largest law firm in the world, the Department of Justice was created in 1789 with a staff of two: an attorney general and a clerk. But that was then, and this is now. Today the Department of Justice is a megapower with its headquarters in Washington DC at the Robert F. Kennedy Building, occupying a city block bordered by Ninth and Tenth Streets and Pennsylvania and Constitution Avenues, Northwest. The department has field offices in all states and in over one hundred countries. In America, there are ninety-three United States attorneys, most of them having multiple offices in their districts, with armies of skilled prosecutors and legions of FBI agents. General Johnson serves as chief commander and overseer.

The primary purpose of the department's existence is to prevent terror and promote the nation's security consistent with the rule of law. Seeking fair and appropriate punishment for those who threaten the citizens and security of America, especially those using terrorist tactics and committing mass murder (bombings, burning of cities, and downing of planes fit those criteria), was the ultimate end game. General Johnson had every intention of giving this unidentified man his day in court and due process; that was her philosophy. She also had no intention of losing the case in a court of law, and that was also her philosophy, especially since this one would be tried on the world stage.

Within weeks of her swearing in, which had not been that long ago, General Johnson was presented with her first challenge, a matter in hot dispute at the White House and the CIA. It had spilled over into the halls of Congress and consequently put the media into a feeding frenzy. The philosophic and legal battle lines had been drawn in a debate as to whether CIA agents could or should be indicted for alleged crimes of torture.

The report that came out of the Senate Intelligence Committee on the use of torture by agents in the field following the 9/11 attacks was scathing, with harrowing excerpts from the CIA interrogation account; to wit, ice water baths and sixty-six hours of standing sleep deprivation (prisoners were kept standing by chaining them to a wall). Photo images were included of detainees chained to the ceiling, clothed in a diaper, and enduring involuntary rectal feeding and rectal hydration, waterboarding, and claustrophobia-inducing confinement in a coffin box for over a week at a time.

General Johnson was taken aback by the graphics since she had never been exposed to anything like that in Downtown Pittsburgh. This was an issue she never before had to deal with morally, let alone legally. She understood the president's position that the report had to be made public and that many mistakes could be made in the rush to justice. She understood Senator John McCain's position, who had been tortured himself during the Vietnam War, that in the long run, more harm than good comes from torturing detainees.

She also understood the response from the CIA, whether she agreed with it or not, that torture under certain circumstances elicits critical information that saves lives and cities. She was hard-pressed to believe that the authorities, or President Bush and Vice President Dick Cheney, could have been in the dark about such matters.

The court of public opinion was mixed as to whether agents should be prosecuted by her office for crimes or whether they should be prosecuted by the International Court of Justice at the Hague for war crimes. General Johnson had to make the call and decided not to indict. She came under much criticism for the first time experiencing the enormous pressures under which Eric Holder had lived. The press conference she held was not limited to KDKA in Pittsburgh or Pittsburgh's *Post-Gazette* and *Tribune-Review*.

When Liam Spokane laid out the history of his investigation, which included photographs of the "man with no name," everyone in that conference room was stunned. These folks figured they had seen it all, but incontrovertible evidence of one individual's presence at five catastrophic sites, including 9/11, over a period of thirteen years, was a bit much. The meeting started out with everyone in the room except Spokane and Johnson taking notes but ended with every attendee just listening in awe.

"Well done," General Johnson said when Spokane had finished speaking. "We'll keep classified what must be classified and make known what must be made known going forward. You'll be kept personally informed of our decisions because when the terrorist world finds out whom we have in our custody, who knows what will happen?"

"Thank you," Spokane answered.

"My first strategic decision is to decide who is to prosecute this man, who will be referred to as John Doe on the indictment, and that decision will determine where the trial will take place geographically. I have three excellent options, but there is one in particular who seems to be exceptionally well suited."

"Who is it?" Spokane asked, not one for fooling around.

"Samuel Nelson in Harrisburg, and here's why. New Jersey has jurisdiction over the plane that crashed in New Jersey and has Russian agents crawling all over the place. I want to keep them out of it because they have their own agenda. John Rivero in New York is a heavy hitter, but I don't want the trial to take place in Manhattan. I don't know what our prisoner's supporters are capable of doing, but it's not going to be done in New York City. Sam Nelson and Fran Korsakov can do this. Besides, the name Korsakov has a nice Russian ring to it, and Harrisburg is not New York."

CHAPTER 13

THE CHOSEN ONE

THE PERSONAL CALL from the United States attorney general directing Sam Nelson to come to Washington DC for a debriefing was like getting a call to appear at the Academy Awards in Hollywood. At least to him it was, and he would dress the part. He went out and bought a three-piece charcoal suit, a contrasting bold red tie, and a pair of wing tips. He was asked to bring FAUSA Fran Korsakov with him.

On November 5, 2015, the two invitees arrived half an hour early for the 9:00 a.m. appointment at the Robert F. Kennedy Building's main office. Because the drive from Harrisburg was only 2.5 hours, and even with a reserved government parking space and escort upon arrival, they began their trip at 5:15 a.m. Fran drove his personal black Jeep Cherokee, newly waxed and polished.

General Katherine Johnson had just finished her morning exercise routine at the in-house gym, and she was ready for the day. Again, she sat at the head of her conference room table, and again, her elite eight were in attendance. She advised Mr. Nelson that he was "the chosen one" to prosecute this nameless man and then gave him a series of marching orders. Her surprise announcement went through Nelson like an electric shock, so intense that the marching orders were at some risk of escaping his attention.

The defendant, presently being held at a black-hole site, was to be indicted by a federal grand jury in Harrisburg, but the formal charging document was to be limited in setting forth the evidence.

He would be referred to as "John Doe" in the indictment.

There would be no bail set, a requirement so obvious that everyone in attendance laughed.

Once indicted, the defendant would be transported under heavy security to the Dauphin County Prison and held there until trial, and security would continue in that county facility at federal government expense. The defendant was to suffer no harm at the hands of prison officials or other inmates.

The Defendant was to have counsel appointed if he could not afford one.

The Defendant was to be tried as soon as possible without compromising his pretrial rights.

Mr. Nelson was to provide her office with weekly memos on the status of the case.

Any press conference following the indictment would be his duty, but every word would be written out ahead of time and approved by her office. The identity and role of the defendant was still under investigation, and not knowing either of these facts, Johnson did not want to set off World War III in the terrorist world by conducting a Department of Justice press conference in Harrisburg.

"One more condition, Sam," General Johnson said sternly.

"The answer is 'Yes, General,' whatever it is," Sam answered respectfully.

General Johnson continued, "This guy is a world terrorist who will be showcased in the American criminal justice system. America will watch this trial and so will the terrorist world. Don't you lose this one, Sam, or you'll be going into private practice. Do you understand?"

"Of course, I understand," he answered smiling. "And don't worry . . . It sounds like a slam dunk."

Sam Nelson's answer and jovial tone annoyed the general, and she took strong exception. She reminded her "chosen one" that there are no slam dunks in the courtroom, that anything can happen. She agreed that the defendant's presence at five disastrous terror attack sites over a thirteen-year period represented a wealth of incriminating evidence, and especially with a Harrisburg jury, he should win the case. But in order to impress this seasoned prosecutor further, she hastened to add that some rookie or hotshot attorney may well argue that mere presence at a crime scene is not enough.

"One reason I picked you over equally qualified United States attorneys in New Jersey and New York," she declared, "is because Harrisburg juries are an easy sell for the United States government. There will be no sympathy in Harrisburg for a mass murderer who burned State Street down and was a possible ISIS leader, so you should be okay. Just don't under-try it."

"I won't lose this case, General Johnson," Nelson said, assuring her, afraid that she might retract her decision.

She nodded, signifying that the meeting was over. With all appropriate security measures in place, the FBI would deliver a copy of the file in its entirety to Nelson at his office in Harrisburg within twenty-four hours. Much of that file was highly classified and was not to see the light of day. With the rampage going on in Washington as a result of the Senate Intelligence Committee's torture report, any measures used during interrogation on the "man with no name" could be misinterpreted.

* * *

The grand jury indictment in the case of *United States of America v. John Doe*, Criminal No. 05-CR-666 (Chief Judge James), was certain and swift, handed down on November 17, 2015. The indictment alleged that the defendant committed acts of mass murder and terrorism on February 9, 2015, causing the deaths of eleven American citizens and serious bodily injury to fifteen others. The indictment further alleged that the defendant committed an act of arson in the burning of State Street, completely destroying eleven buildings all within one block at the foot of the Capitol and destroying forty-two parked cars, causing at least an estimated $500 million worth of damage. Reckless endangerment to others was added to the host of charges as was obstruction of justice.

Grand jury proceedings consist of twenty-three citizens who are sworn in by a federal judge for the purpose of listening to one-sided evidence presented by a federal prosecutor. After hearing the evidence, it falls upon that grand jury to decide whether or not to charge the named or unnamed suspect with the crimes he was alleged to have committed. The federal government's burden relates to probable cause versus proof beyond a reasonable doubt. Neither the defendant nor his counsel are present at this closed-chamber proceeding, nor are defense witnesses called or made known to the grand jury.

Indictments are considered a slam dunk. If you "can indict a ham sandwich," an assessment coined by New York State chief judge Sol Wachtler on how easy it is to indict someone, the "man with no name" was the whole ham in Harrisburg.

No bail for "John Doe" was also a sure thing. When he was taken in handcuffs and shackles before a federal magistrate in Downtown Harrisburg and refused to identify himself or his country, there was nothing to talk about.

A trial date was set for March 2016. All pretrial motions were to be filed by mid-January. The appointment of counsel for the defendant would be made by a federal district court judge because of the high stakes involved. The government was seeking the death penalty, and Sam Nelson had already gotten the required approval and blessing from the United States Attorney General's Office in Washington.

Once the defendant was denied bail and relocated under maximum security to his new home at Dauphin County Prison, the indictment of *United States v. John Doe* was unsealed. The public relations office out of Washington, not Harrisburg, released that indictment to the media. There were no leaks before that, and once this charging document hit the media's desks, there was blood in the water, and the sharks moved in.

General Kathleen Johnson had agreed to have United States attorney Sam Nelson do the international press conference. Since it was a Harrisburg case, the case was his. By prearrangement, the attorney general's office in Washington had already edited and approved the written draft he'd submitted, and he was ordered not to go off script. Every reference about wolves was deleted, and the speech itself was significantly abbreviated. He was not to answer any questions, no matter how many were asked.

The media is the loudest voice and theater in America. "For Congress shall pass no law abridging the freedom of speech." Its societal and political force is omnipresent and so powerful that it has been referred to as the Fourth Estate. Advances in technology have made it more possible than at any other time in history for events and speeches to be seen and heard globally with lightning speed. Broadcasts are transmitted in high definition; even Hollywood can't touch their creativity. Media is no longer limited to a newspaper on the porch or a daily half-hour network broadcast. Now it has enormous ability to shape opinion and thought through its televised twenty-four-hour, nonstop news cycle and Internet access.

This Fourth Estate, this voice and theater, can be accurate in its presentation or not. This mind-shaping institution can rise to the level of brainwashing. It can be very entertaining, informative, and educational on one hand but destructive and frightening on the other. The media can be your friend one day and turn on you the next, like a ravenous jackal. Media members can also turn on each other, often to make a show of strength, power, and wealth. The media doesn't care if you are an individual or an institution. They are nondiscriminatory and unpredictable.

Ask those who have been in power one day and out the next.

Today there is a force that will soon be the Fifth Estate, maybe more powerful than the fourth. It is the electronic world making such rapid advances that it must be confronted. It is the world of computers, smartphones, Twitter, bloggers, Facebook, Instagram, and an expanding array of apps and news reporting sites. Whether you are picking a jury in a small town or having an international press conference such as the one on Sam Nelson's schedule, you must be aware of these new ways of communicating that affect us all.

Sam Nelson's romance with the media in the past had been mainly local, but having said that, he had good relations with them, at least to date. He was the United States attorney for the Middle District and a resource to whom the reporters typically went for information. His style was authoritative, at times friendly, and other times businesslike; occasionally, he would inject humor into his press conferences but not often, since crimes against the United States government aren't funny. There was no room for humor in his prepared remarks in the case of *United States v. John Doe.*

He had carefully chosen the site for this press conference. He would speak from the top of the Capitol Building steps overlooking the ravaged State Street. Both American and Pennsylvania flags would be his props, arranged behind him at the podium. On his right, he was flanked by the attorney general of Pennsylvania; AUSA Fran Korsakov; FBI SA Valerie Sing, assistant to Wilson; and FBI SA Bill Wilson, who had worked on the case previously and was his friend. On his left stood the governor of Pennsylvania, the lieutenant governor, a senator pro tem, and Harrisburg's mayor. Behind this cast of characters was another cluster of dignitaries, which included the speaker of the Pennsylvania House, a Dauphin County district attorney, the commissioner of the Pennsylvania State Police, and others. There were many phone calls and favors cashed in to be part of this production.

The time was 11:00 a.m. Eastern time.

The date was December 7, 2015, the seventieth anniversary of Pearl Harbor.

The early winter morning in Downtown Harrisburg was chilly, but the sun was shining, and there was no wind. Samuel Nelson walked out of the Capitol Building right on time, and the dignitaries in attendance made way for him to get to the podium. This was his biggest press conference ever, and he hoped he was ready for it. The expansive steps of the Capitol below him were filled with a phalanx of cameras and microphones. He noted that the biggest networks in America were there and the biggest newspapers—the *New York Times, Washington Post, Chicago Tribune, Philadelphia Inquirer, Los Angeles Times,* and *Atlanta Journal Constitution*—after that, he lost count. Folks from everywhere were in attendance, having learned about this conference. They were relegated to stand on State Street, which had been cordoned off for crowd control. A helicopter hovered, and armed Pennsylvania State Police lined the streets.

Gen. Kathleen Allen Johnson and many of her staff were watching the event on a TV in her office.

"You better not go off script," she said talking to herself, but her staff heard her.

Sam Nelson gripped the podium, took a deep but controlled breath, and delivered exactly as he had rehearsed at home time and time again.

Harrisburg, Pennsylvania—"On November 17 of this year, a federal grand jury in Harrisburg indicted a man the United States government believes is responsible for the act of terrorism committed in Harrisburg at the foot of the steps from where I speak. He has been charged with the February 9, 2015, burning and bombing of State Street that caused the deaths of eleven American citizens and brought about serious bodily injury to fifteen others. He has also been charged with arson, said fire completely destroying eleven buildings all within one block. The estimated cost of damage is over $500 million. He has also been charged with reckless endangerment and obstruction of justice.

Evidence set forth in the indictment puts this man at the foot of the Twin Tower buildings on September 11, 2001; puts this man at the subway of the transit bombing in London on July 7, 2007; puts this man in Macy's at the bombing and burning of that department store on Black Friday last year; puts this man at the site of the downed plane that crashed and burned in the Pine Barrens of New Jersey. And finally, our evidence will show that he was present here in Harrisburg watching State Street burn.

The government believes that the man we have in custody at this time, who will be held without bail until his trial date next March, is a key figure in these aforesaid atrocities that have terrorized London and America. The investigation is continuing, and further progress is being made.

This is America. The United States government will afford this man due process, but the end result will be justice. We will be seeking the death penalty for the mass murder of American citizens on American soil.

I want to thank the men and women in the Department of Counterterrorism who helped apprehend this suspect. I also want to express my sincere appreciation for the tireless efforts of the Federal Bureau of Investigation and Central Intelligence Agency. Last, but certainly not least, I want to thank the Pennsylvania State Police for their invaluable support.

Because this far-reaching investigation continues, I will not be answering any questions from the media at this time. I promise America, however, that all questions will be answered in due course, no later than March, and from the courtroom floor.

Thank you all for attending."

Cameras continued to roll as he shook hands with dignitaries in attendance.

"He did it," General Johnson told her staff, pleased with the script and the delivery.

Within minutes, the photograph of John Doe was circulated around the world. It was one that would be featured on the front page of every newspaper in the country by morning and the cover of *Time Magazine* by the end of the week.

CHAPTER 14

FSB

December 8, 2015
The Kremlin
Moscow, Russia

VLADIMIR PUTIN, PRESIDENT of Russia since 2012, was a proud man with an attitude. His "White House" was the Kremlin in Moscow, a historic fortress with five palaces, four cathedrals, and the enclosing Kremlin Wall with Kremlin Towers. The complex, an architectural wonder built in the 1400s and expanded over time, still served as the official residence of the president of the Russian Federation.

In 2015, Vladimir Putin was sixty-two years old and an increasingly isolated president on a mission to restore his country's lost empire. He had been an officer for sixteen years in the KGB, which was the Soviet's feared secret police and intelligence agency, with enforcement powers that would be unacceptable in the Free World. Foreign observers viewed him as an undemocratic dictator. He was five feet seven inches tall and often compared to Napoleon because of their similar complexes and philosophies.

On the day the indictment was announced in America, he was in his vast war room with the director of the FSB, Army General Alexander Bortnikov. The mirrors in the room were floor to ceiling and the massive chandeliers pure crystal. Antique tapestries lined the walls, and ornate baroque furniture filled the room. It was a space befitting the czars of Russia and the current president as well.

The FSB was Russia's current strong-arm branch of government, responsible for intelligence gathering, espionage, and counterespionage;

its security; and their war against terrorism. This organization employed over 200,000, but the exact number was a state secret. Another estimate stated there were 66,200 uniformed staff, a number which included about 4,000 highly trained special forces troops. General Bortnikov ran this machine with an iron fist, a tyrant in his own right. In fact, the year he became director of the FSB, the American Carnegie *Foreign Policy* magazine named Russia as "the worst place to be a terrorist" and highlighted Russia's willingness to set national security above civil rights.

These two men of power and authority watched America's press conference together and looked at each other cynically when it was over.

General Alexander Bortnikov was dressed in a Russian military uniform with knee-high black leather boots. Stars accented his gold epaulets, and the medallions pinned neatly on his right pocket confirmed that he was battle worn. His long curled mustache was neatly trimmed and waxed. He had removed his braided cap for his conference and discussion with the president of his country.

President Vladimir Putin was both unimpressed and skeptical over America's "partnership role" in getting to the bottom of the Russian Airbus crash. America returned the bodies and personal property to Russia with order and dignity, but Putin wasn't buying into America's theory that ISIS was the culprit. He had the picture of the suspect the morning after the plane went down, killing sixty-four of Russia's wealthiest and most esteemed people, but then America would not allow Putin's people access to him.

Putin would have liked his interrogators an opportunity to use their own "enhanced techniques" on this man and was sure their methods would have been a little more productive. Giving a suspect a little extra water while strapped to a board, or denying him a full night's sleep, or letting him rest too long in a coffin was not the Russian definition of enhancement. Even before the crash of the plane, the Americans were upset at these measures used after 9/11 because their Senate Intelligence Committee had determined those measures to be immoral and ineffective.

If Putin and Bortnikov had "John Doe," he would have been taken to Lubyanka, the Central Moscow building notorious during the Soviet era for interrogations in its basement cells. Those cells are still intact, as well as the necessary tools: drills for bones, saws for cutting, hot irons for eyes, hand clippers for gonads. The Americans can debate the morality of torture, but the Russians never do . . . because with the right tools, it works.

Then there is the indictment handed down in America that infuriated Putin. First, the Americans charge the man they apprehended, who, in a way, basically told them to go fuck themselves. Then they have a press conference promising the world that he will be given due process, which is what the law does for drunk drivers. And even if they're right that their suspect is a world terrorist—something Putin agreed with—the Americans still didn't have a clue as to who crashed the plane, or who bombed Macy's, or who burned Harrisburg, or how any of this was accomplished.

To Putin, that's not promised justice to the American people; that's a fucking joke.

Since the crash in the New Jersey Pine Barrens on October 16, 2015, the Russians were doing their own investigation and weren't sharing information with America, just as America wasn't sharing information with Russia. There was one exception, however, where the two world powers compared notes and agreed with each other: the cause of the crash.

The Federal Aviation Administration is very good at what they do, and that is determining the cause of airplane crashes.

But the FSB is also very good at what they do, and they also determine the cause of airplane crashes. The branch responsible for that within the FSB has long taken on "computer geeks" and their like in order to stay ahead of the game. These bright young experts come from the country's top technology institutes, and the best of them are invited to apply. The vetting process of these students is exhaustive because of the classified nature of what they do.

The agreed-upon result between the FAA and the FSB? The 300 series Airbus was hot-wired. That plane's complex and coded computer system is the brain and command center of the controls. That brain and command center was accessed by a superhacker after he got past the classified code, which is not an easy task.

Hot-wiring the computer also requires technological sophistication. Once the system is entered and the controls are taken over remotely, the pilots are rendered helpless, and the plane can be taken wherever the remote operator decides for it to land or crash. This procedure is called "fly by wire."

The United States and Russia both agreed that "fly by wire" is what happened to the 300 series Airbus.

The United States attorney in America and the United States government still thought ISIS was behind it. Putin, on the other hand, never believed those guys who cut heads off with kitchen knives on television, and ran around in old pickup trucks, had one guy in their ranks who was capable of such an act. He had executed those five who were seen on television claiming responsibility just for shooting their mouths off not because he really believed they did it.

Putin was also convinced ISIS was not responsible for another reason: when a plane is hotwired, its destination can be controlled. This plane did not miss a target the size of Manhattan; this plane crashed at a site in the United States that brought no harm to Americans on purpose. In other words, whoever did this act hated Russians and loved Americans.

Therefore, not ISIS.

Putin also eliminated America as a suspect.

First of all, Americans don't believe in terrorism. It is beneath their dignity and morality as a nation, and they are proud of that pedestal they occupy. They don't even believe in torture, at least not anymore, for the same reasons. America does their killing by bombing thousands of people at a time with air strikes. They shocked and awed the world with their fireworks in Iraq and reduced Baghdad to ashes.

Since the beheading of two of their journalists, they had launched over three thousand air strikes targeting ISIS strongholds, killing thousands more.

Americans would rather kill from afar with high-tech mechanized drones.

These American-style killings, which take thousands of innocent lives, including those of small children, are written off as collateral damage, a cost of doing war . . . therefore, moral and ethical.

"They are fucking hypocrites," Putin told his general, who was in total agreement.

General Bortnikov had seen the wrath of American air strikes from the ground, during the NATO bombing in Serbia and then again in Afghanistan after 9/11. The screaming American fighter jets with their firepower brought their own sense of terror to mankind. Years ago, when he was a young soldier, he had the opportunity to tour what the scourge of napalm did to Vietnam.

"They are fucking hypocrites," the general reiterated and said nothing more.

Putin also eliminated America from a short list of suspects because the Airbus to America was carrying Russia's elite businessmen and investors. The scheduled conference was embraced by America's economic giants, and the economy in that country needed a boost. This contingent from Russia was going to do that, and they were going to make those Americans a lot of money. Wall Street had too much money and power invested in the political system. To Putin, Americans love their money and would not have acted against their own interests by crashing that plane.

There was, however, one suspect in Putin's crosshairs.

* * *

In late February 2014, Russia began to send unmarked military equipment and troops into Ukraine in what has been termed a *stealth invasion*. London-based military experts and the U.S. State Department said the soldiers were likely Russian special forces and airborne units. The world believed that Putin was on the move to reclaim Ukraine, which many Russians considered to be the ancient precursor to the modern-day Russian Federation; indeed, its capital of Kiev was often called the "mother city of Russia."

Russia had openly annexed Crimea, a peninsula in the Black Sea, which historically was controlled by Russia and given to Ukraine on a whim by Khrushchev in the 1950s.

Putin's public position was that all the people of Ukraine were crying for reentry.

The Free World saw it differently and viewed it as an overt act of aggression that would further Putin's mission to restore his country's lost empire. NATO increasingly saw Russia as a dangerous force but did nothing. Meanwhile, the United States was beleaguered worldwide in its fight against terrorism and increasing its efforts to protect U.S. borders; therefore, it did not put boots on the ground in Ukraine. However, on March 4, 2014, the United States pledged $1 billion in aid to that country.

Much bloodshed was spilled on both sides of the battle line.

On July 17, 2014, there was more bloodshed to come. Malaysian Airlines Flight 17 was a scheduled international passenger flight from Amsterdam to Kuala Lumpur, the capital of Malaysia. It was shot down from the ground, killing all 283 passengers and fifteen crew members on board, over territory controlled by pro-Russian Ukrainian separatists. Russia denied responsibility, but Ukrainians still loyal to their government are convinced otherwise.

Many countries thereafter implemented economic sanctions against Russia and Russian individuals and companies, to which Russia responded in kind.

To President Vladimir Putin, the crash of the 300 series Airbus carrying no one but Russians was a terrorist act that he ordered the FSB to investigate in this context. Investigate it they did, and on orders from Putin himself, the power and might of this ruthless agency were unleashed. His prime suspect was Ukraine, and because of the sophistication required to hack a Russian-owned and -protected codified computer, the focus of the investigation narrowed considerably.

The FSB boys, with their own computerized search engine capacities, checked every educational institution in the world to find that limited number who would be capable. Once they came up with the list, they resorted to their old methods of searches and seizures and interrogations using enhanced techniques. Even as President Putin and General Bortnikov sat in the Kremlin's war room on December 8, 2015, the culprits they believed were responsible had been identified but were still at large.

The guilty parties were a team of six hackers, each one of them capable of the sophistication required to hot-wire that Airbus. They were all Ukrainian by descent, all Eastern Orthodox by religion, and Putin intended to send them to their lord. His search to find them would continue, and it would be relentless.

CHAPTER 15

LAWYERED UP

THE HONORABLE JUDGE Joseph Andrew James looked at the petition for the appointment of counsel filed by the Federal Public Defender's Office in Harrisburg. Judge James was the assigned judge to the case of *United States v. John Doe*, a case scheduled for trial by jury in his courtroom in mid-March 2016, less than four months away. He actually assigned the case to himself because he wanted it, and since he was the chief judge of the Middle District, he could make it happen.

The petition alleged that "John Doe" was without means to retain counsel, was indigent as a matter of law, and under the Sixth Amendment to the United States Constitution had a right to the effective assistance of counsel. It also requested expenses for an investigator and expert witnesses. The petition was signed by the senior attorney in the Federal Public Defender's Office Frank Carlucci, who had been with that office for eighteen years.

Judge James had been on the bench a long time, and because federal judges have a lifetime appointment with no mandatory retirement, he was still there. At seventy-three, having been a lifetime chain-smoker, his age and frailty were beginning to show. His thinning white hair was distinguished-looking, but the deep wrinkles on his face made him look older than he was. His hands trembled slightly when they were not resting, an indication of his delicate health. He had received treatment for lung cancer and assured that it was successful, but the experience had put the fear of God in him.

And God was an important part of his life. He was a religious man, for without his beliefs, nothing made sense. While Judge James may still have had a lot of unanswered questions, those that had been resolved for him by his beliefs had truly strengthened his faith. He was a Catholic, and his church was St. Patrick's Cathedral on State Street. Although the fire had not reached that Gothic stone edifice and house of worship, it had come dangerously close.

He had been married for fifty-one years, but his wife passed away in 2011. His two grown sons' marriages had produced three small grandchildren, but with the exception of an occasional token phone call, there was very little contact, and they never visited. His judicial position precluded any meaningful friendships, and so he was often lonely.

Judge James, like everybody else in the legal community, was reading the newspapers and following the "John Doe" case on the Internet. The State Street fire not only had almost reached his church but the conflagration also had occurred only three blocks from the federal courthouse where he presided. He remembered the night of the fire as though it were yesterday, for he had gotten a call from his law clerk at 1:30 a.m. telling him that Harrisburg was burning down and to turn on the news to see it. He watched the fire rage from his living room and saw terror in the faces of the people who had braved the cold night to observe.

Though aging and with substantial health concerns, Judge James was still a true legal scholar, having written legal opinions that would be the law for years to come. He was a trial judge and insisted on decorum and respect in his courtroom, with little patience for histrionics from lawyers. Although he afforded the government due respect, he was not their rubber stamp. There were a lot of defense lawyers who annoyed him, but sometimes he felt that some of that was because of his feeling about their guilty clients who had forever ruined the lives of their victims.

Judge James, like everyone else, was taken aback by the alleged facts in the indictment. It took a lot to shock this judge, for he had seen it all in the well of his courtroom. But the allegations that "John Doe" was at five catastrophic crime scenes in two different countries over a thirteen-year period . . . carnage brought about by acts of terror that will forever go down in history . . . *Wow!* In his experience, a conviction in the Middle District of Pennsylvania was certain, justice would be swift, and the death penalty would be imposed in less than an hour of deliberations.

Judge James did not believe in the death penalty; he maintained that it was not the government's right to impose this penalty in a court of law. This sanction was for a higher order. Judge James believed in heaven, and he believed in hell. Nevertheless, the death penalty was the law of the land, challenged in the Supreme Court of the United States and affirmed, and Judge James would abide by the law. He had imposed the death penalty one time in his career, and it troubled him deeply, but he was prepared to do it again.

With a stroke of the pen, he granted the petition on his desk and ordered that it be sealed. The defendant would be represented by Frank Carlucci who would try the case in chief. The defendant would have a second lawyer who was death-qualified, taken from a list of death-qualified lawyers who had volunteered to undertake such a task when assigned. That lawyer would be Stephanie Jackson, an eminently qualified young African American lawyer who taught criminal law at Shippensburg University in Shippensburg, Pennsylvania. Judge James liked both lawyers but knew that Stephanie had nothing to work with, for there would be no mitigating circumstances to outweigh the aggravating nature of the crimes, and there would be no mercy.

Judge James also dictated an order that had not been requested, with a copy to the United States attorney, directing the warden at the Dauphin County Prison to make the prisoner available to his counsel at all times, consistent with appropriate security measures, in a private room at the prison, "and the integrity of said room was not to be violated." Judge James did not want any electronic eavesdropping that would compromise this case in any way.

* * *

Frank Carlucci and Stephanie Jackson waited in the assigned room at the Dauphin County Prison for their client to be brought in. Both lawyers knew this was the kind of case in which very few lawyers in the world would ever have the chance to participate. They were excited at the opportunity and willing to incur wrath from the court of public opinion that comes with representing heinous criminals. They were prepared to investigate all leads, if any, and had already discussed the mountain of motions they intended to file. They would seek all

WILLIAM C. COSTOPOULOS

discovery above and beyond what would be provided, classified or not. They would seek a change of venue. They would request individual voir dire (in this case, a vow by jurors to tell the truth). They would seek to suppress evidence, and they would seek one continuance after another to delay picking the jury for as long as possible.

Carlucci came from an Italian background and had represented a lot of Mafia-related cases. He joined the Federal Public Defender's Office after a short stint in practice and had tried a lot of cases over eighteen years, but most of his work was entering guilty pleas and working the sentencing guidelines. He looked a lot like a young Frank Sinatra, and his first name suited him well.

Finally, the knock on the door came, and it was time to get down to work.

The prisoner walked in with no restraints, dressed in an orange jumpsuit with "DCP" on the back. Without invitation, he sat down at the metal table where Frank and Stephanie were already seated and waiting. Frank attempted to shake hands, but his client did not reciprocate. It was an awkward moment for the two lawyers.

Frank began with a speech he had made many times over the years by rote. "Sir, my name is Frank Carlucci, and I'm the senior federal public defender here in Harrisburg. I've been appointed to represent you and have been doing this for a long time, eighteen years to be exact. I'm here with Prof. Stephanie Jackson, also a lawyer, and she'll be assisting me in your representation.

"Anything you say to us in this room falls within the attorney-client privilege and will be kept confidential. We have obtained a separate court order directing that this conference room's integrity not be violated, and we don't believe this room is wired. We'll be filing pretrial motions on your behalf at the appropriate time, and your trial date is scheduled for March.

"We'll be your lawyers throughout and advising you throughout.

"Do you have any questions for us before we begin?" Carlucci asked, wrapping up his speech.

Their client signaled that he had none.

"What is your name, sir?" Carlucci asked, and with that, Stephanie picked up her pen to write on her pad.

Their client shook his head once again, still silent. Neither Carlucci nor Stephanie had ever before found themselves in such a situation.

"Why won't you give us your name?" Carlucci asked, incredulous. And with that, their client gave them a speech they would never forget.

"Pay attention," their client began. "You are my lawyers, and I thank you for that. You'll do what I ask, or I'll seek a change of counsel. I am the client, and here's how we're going to do it. You are to file no pretrial motions whatsoever. You are to engage in no investigation. You are to seek no continuances. This case is to be tried in March as scheduled. Once the government rests its case, you are to call me to the witness stand, and I will do the rest. Do you have any questions?"

Both Carlucci and Jackson were stunned as if each had been drenched with a bucket of ice water. Neither of them was ready for *this*, and neither of them knew what to say.

Their client spoke again in an effort, it seemed, to help them out.

"There is no need to see me again. I'll continue to be here, at all times on good behavior. If you deem it necessary to file a motion for a psychiatric evaluation, go ahead, although it's unnecessary. Please let your psychiatrist know that I won't be taking any tests or agreeing to any examinations. Just be prepared to try this case consistent with my wishes. You will not be getting a report that will give rise to an insanity defense but rather one that states I am competent to stand trial. Thank you very much, and have a good day," he said and ended the interview just like that.

Before he exited the room after knocking to bring the guards to the door, he turned and made one final remark for his lawyers. "Nothing personal."

* * *

Frank Carlucci immediately filed, under seal, with the Honorable Judge Joseph James a petition for a psychiatric evaluation without setting forth any reasons. The petition requested that it be kept under seal and not made known to the government at this time.

Judge James understood the petition and the reasons for it. He certainly didn't want the media getting hold of it, and it was premature for the government to get involved. If "John Doe" was going to assert insanity or incompetency to stand trial through his legal counsel, there would be a hearing in the judge's courtroom, courtroom 1, and the government would then be a party. Judge James promptly signed the order.

Within days of counsel's visit to the prison, Dr. Lisa Schneider was signing in at the front desk of Dauphin County Prison. She had done this before but was looking forward to meeting her new patient after being debriefed by his lawyers. She looked like she had auditioned to be a psychiatrist in a movie, her face accented with dark-rimmed glasses and her hair in a bun.

Dr. Schneider waited in the assigned room at the Dauphin County Prison for her patient to be brought in. She knew this was an interview that very few psychiatrists in the world would have such an opportunity to undertake. She was excited and thought herself well prepared for her patient's stubbornness brought about by his mental illness; after all, dealing with sociopaths and psychopaths and nonmedicated schizophrenics was her life's work.

Finally, the knock on the door came. As he had previously done, the detainee walked in with no restraints, dressed in an orange jumpsuit with "DCP" on the back, and without invitation seated himself at the metal table where Dr. Schneider was seated and waiting. Dr. Schneider extended her hand to shake his hand, but her patient demurred. "Sir," Dr. Schneider began, a speech she made many times over the years from memory after many such assignments, "my name is Dr. Lisa Schneider, and I am a licensed psychiatrist, certified by the National Board of Psychiatry in America. I've been asked to meet with you at the request of your lawyers to make certain determinations that will be important to you in the upcoming court proceedings. Anything you say to me in this room falls within the doctor-patient privilege and will be kept confidential. Do you understand?"

Her patient nodded affirmatively.

"Do you have any questions for me before we begin?" Dr. Schneider asked, wrapping up her speech.

Her patient shook his head.

"What is your name, sir?" Dr. Schneider asked pro forma.

Her patient said nothing.

"Why won't you give me your name?" she asked her patient.

And with that, her patient gave her a speech that *she* would never forget but would be sufficient for her to do the requested report.

"Dr. Schneider," he said to her, "I'm not going to get into a question-and-answer interview. I know why you're here and what your responsibility is to my lawyers and the court. There are two issues here that you must address. First, to determine whether or not I am competent to stand trial. I can assure you that I meet the standard required to stand trial pursuant to *Dusky v. United States,* a decision handed down by the U.S. Supreme Court. It's an old one but still the law, requiring that I understand the nature of the proceedings and participate rationally in the court process. I understand the government wants to take me to trial for killing a lot of people, that I'm presumed innocent until proven guilty, that they must prove their case beyond a reasonable doubt, and that I'm entitled to the effective assistance of counsel. Now do you have any questions?" he asked his doctor, who was now speechless except for a whispered no.

"Good," her patient answered and continued in a lecturing tone. "Second, you are here to determine whether or not I am legally insane. I can assure you that I am legally sane, and in fact, I have no mental health issues. The test for legal insanity is "Did the defendant know what he was doing or, if so, that it was wrong?" For further explanation of this determination, you might want to review the *McNaughton rule,* a pronouncement that was a reaction to the acquittal in 1843 of Daniel McNaughton on the charge of murdering Edmund Drummond, whom McNaughton had mistaken for the British prime minister Robert Peel.

"Dr. Schneider," he continued, in an attempt to ease his stunned psychiatrist's obvious distress, "Trust me when I tell you that I knew what I was doing at all times and that *I* know the difference between right and wrong. For example, killing people is wrong.

"Is there anything else you need to complete your report?" he asked in summation very politely.

Dr. Schneider shook her head and got the hell out of there.

CHAPTER 16

COFFIN NAILS

ONE OF THE enhanced interrogation techniques exposed by the Senate Intelligence Committee was the harrowing coffin treatment. A noncompliant detainee would be put into diapers and then forced into a coffin with the lid secured to eliminate any movement from within. No amount of crying, begging, pleading, or whimpering would elicit a response from the individual's captors. In one instance, a detainee was kept in that dark, confining, immobilizing box for eleven days.

Such draconian torture, criticized and denounced as "extreme" by the Senate Intelligence Committee, may have also outraged much of the civilized world: America, France, Spain, Germany, even China.

But not AUSA Fran Korsakov.

He was okay with it, believing terrorists brought it on themselves and deserved what they got after 9/11. There was no time for niceties when America was under attack, not knowing if we would be struck again, and there were rumors that the next one could be nuclear.

"They were fucking terrorists!" he told his wife of ten years, angry that she brought it up again. "They fucking killed three thousand people on that day. You would feel differently if one of our children had been on one of those planes or in one of those buildings!"

"I would rather they die than be put in a coffin for almost two weeks and then chained to a wall for thirteen years!" she screamed back, "And from what I read, you don't have shit on this guy other than he was watching!"

The Korsakovs had three young children at home, but their marriage was on the rocks and destined for divorce. Between his hot temper and binge drinking and her constant nagging and fighting back, things had been going from bad to worse. She would be filing a divorce complaint in Dauphin County in the middle of Fran's all-consuming trial preparation in the "John Doe" case.

Fran wouldn't care. He was fucking a pretty young secretary in his office and looking forward to spending more time with her, maybe starting over with somebody who understood him better and who loved the sex, which he was being denied at home. Fran was fanatical about aging, keeping his full head of curly hair dyed black, and the pretty secretary liked that. When she remarked that she didn't like his salt-and-pepper goatee, he shaved it.

Notwithstanding his failed marriage, and the one before that, Fran Korsakov was regarded in the legal community as the consummate trial prosecutor. His preparation for any trial was exhaustive, and he had the resources of the United States government with its unlimited funds, unlimited manpower, and unlimited technical support.

His skill level on the courtroom floor was textbook, especially his cross-examination, and his closing arguments mesmerizing. Though some of his tactics were viewed by many as ethically marginal, he never pretended to be a saint. In the courtroom, business was business, and you did what you had to do.

Fran had never lost a major case, unlike his boss Sam Nelson who was more a politician than a courtroom lawyer—obsessed with press conferences and shaking hands—and who sometimes seemed to be unfocused. Nelson's recent obsession with some lone wolf or wolves theory was causing Fran some stress, but he hoped they would slink away before jury selection.

His most recent argument with his wife really affected him, especially her comment "You don't have shit on this guy other than he was watching!"

She hit a real nerve with that condemnation.

From the time he returned from Washington DC with Nelson, he was losing sleep thinking about Attorney General Johnson's stern reaction to his "This will be a slam dunk" comment, namely, that there were no slam dunks in a trial and to be mindful that some rookie or hotshot lawyer would make an issue of the "mere presence is not

WILLIAM C. COSTOPOULOS

enough" factor. So although everyone in his office and on the street assured him that it would be a slam dunk, he realized he needed to be ready with more than a clean shot into the basket, and anyway, he wanted something that would bring the crowd to their feet . . . and a guaranteed win.

Sam Nelson could practice his opening and closing in front of a mirror all he wanted to, but Fran Korsakov had work to do. The first thing he did was make it known to the Dauphin County district attorney and the warden of Dauphin County Prison that he was in the market for one or more jailhouse confessions. A jailhouse confession is an incriminating statement, if not a complete admission, to a crime made by an incarcerated defendant to a fellow inmate. Dauphin County Prison had been a honey hole in the past for jailhouse confessions, but whether or not such an alleged statement is credible is decided by a jury. There were many defendants convicted in a court of law based on the testimony of snitches, paid for by the prosecution.

The inmate's reward for coming forward, and Fran made it clear that he would be willing to deal, would be reduced charges for the inmate and a sweet sentence. That many of these prisoners were committing perjury in exchange for early if not immediate release while prosecutors simply turned a blind eye has been commonly accepted as part of the American criminal justice system.

Immediately, the prosecutor's comment about willingness to deal began to spread through the prison system just like the fire on State Street.

Also, you don't try cases for eighteen years without a bank of experts to call to the witness stand. Federal government experts are often retained and paid hefty fees to present their opinions in a court of law. The federal government also has its own experts on the payroll, working in the various bureaucratic offices in Washington DC and in its crime labs: forensic pathologists for cause and manner of death, forensic psychiatrists for the defendant's state of mind, forensic accountants to do the math, and fingerprint and blood experts for positive identification.

The crime labs of the United States federal government are the best in the world. The most esteemed lab is located at the marine corps base in Quantico, Virginia. Many movies such as *Silence of the Lambs* starring Anthony Hopkins and TV series like *CSI* are based on this institution's activities and achievements. It's a department within the

United States Federal Bureau of Investigation that provides forensic analysis support services to the FBI and therefore to the United States Attorney's Office prosecuting the cases. Their courtroom testimony is given great weight.

Fran had worked with that lab many times over a span of almost two decades. There was a certain serologist there whom he had used in the past and could sure use again now. Her name was Jennifer Janson, a 2004 graduate of Michigan State University and whose PhD dissertation was on DNA. She had worked for the federal government in Quantico's crime lab since earning her doctorate. Dr. Janson was no bleeding-heart liberal and like Fran was a firm believer that if you do the crime, you do the time.

One week before Christmas, he made the call, asking to see her personally to avoid the risk of talking on the phone.

"Why the personal visit?" Janson asked, half teasing. She knew that Fran had a playboy reputation and that he was attracted to her. She was fine with that but never had allowed him to cross the line. Getting a job with the FBI crime lab in Quantico was no easy task, and the code of conduct at that institution left little room for poor judgment.

"This is big," Fran answered, "And that's why . . . It's about our boy with no name, the one we've got behind bars up there in Pennsylvania."

Jennifer Janson knew exactly the individual to whom Fran was referring—who didn't?—a mysterious individual believed to be the most evil terrorist and human being and one who had brought death and destruction to thousands throughout the world. She had been looking forward to meeting with Fran and getting involved in the case but was determined to let him know she had questions about where this was going.

"I'll tell you where this is going," Fran told Jennifer in a private conference room as Jennifer listened intently.

"You know what this case is about and that we must win this one. I was told that personally by the attorney general herself. We have a good case, but it would sure be nice if John Doe's DNA were on that bomb on State Street. Your lab has what's left of that bomb, and you have John Doe's blood samples."

"What are you asking?" Janson asked.

"I . . . It's not that I'm asking for anything . . . It's just that it would help the government's case if you would look into a DNA match . . . And it would be the final nail needed to close the coffin permanently."

"I understand," she responded knowingly.

And Dr. Janson did understand, for she had done it before. Sometimes for certain levels of evil, the end justifies the means. Fran Korsakov was not asking for a coffin nail; he was asking for a stake that he could thrust into the heart of a Dracula-like figure, who was now sitting in the Dauphin County Prison.

* * *

The days continued to tick away, and the March trial was fast approaching.

No pretrial motions had been filed, and that was unusual, especially in a death penalty case. No continuance was asked for, which wasn't Frank Carlucci's style or how his office was known to operate.

A separate room was set up in the United States Attorney's Office in Harrisburg as headquarters for the "John Doe" case. Only Nelson, Korsakov, and the assigned FBI agents had keys. There were time lines and charts on the walls. Diagrams had been prepared, accurately specifying in feet and inches where John Doe had been standing at each of the crime scenes. Color photos were displayed on easels so the jury could grasp the horrific extent of each catastrophe. Other similar photos placing John Doe at all five sites beyond a reasonable doubt had been blown up poster size for maximum visualization (the one of him standing on the church steps watching the towers burn was the most sinister).

Sam Nelson was spending all his time on this case and turned over other responsibilities that came with his office to a veteran assistant U.S. attorney. There were many other cases pending that needed attention. In addition, there were administrative duties: bickering personnel who required conflict resolution, incoming and outgoing calls to be processed appropriately, and correspondence to be dictated, typed, and mailed, and Sam Nelson was too busy for any of this.

Then two calls came in to Fran Korsakov that he had been anticipating: one from Dauphin County Prison (there were two different inmates who wanted to see him) and one from the Quantico crime lab stating that a package with an expert opinion contained therein was waiting for pickup.

The case of *United States v. John Doe* was now ready to be tried.

CHAPTER 17

PRECAUTIONS

JOHN RIVERO HAD never met Pres. Vladimir Putin, had no need to, never wanted to, never intended to, and never would.

But just as President Putin believed that America's case in Harrisburg answered no questions—questions like Who actually committed these terrorist acts? Was there a common enemy at the different attack sites? And how were these attacks all accomplished?—John Rivero was asking himself the same ones. He was the sitting United States attorney for Manhattan and had a bombing in his city at Macy's that went off on three different floors, and his city—the Big Apple—had been very jittery since 9/11.

Of the Macy's bombing that killed 105 people, 32 were children, and 240 were taken to intensive care. The official investigation known as MACBOMB was intense enough to generate thirty thousand interviews and one billion pieces of information, but to date, the perpetrator or perpetrators were as yet unknown. It might be a good idea, by his way of thinking, to find that out.

To that end, he got no help from Liam Spokane and that contingent from Washington DC.

Neither did he get any help from Sam Nelson in Harrisburg, who was still convinced that one terrorist was responsible.

Rivero also knew that Russia didn't give a shit that Americans shopping for Christmas presents had been killed at Macy's.

So he, John Rivero, having done it throughout his reign as the sitting United States attorney in the Southern District, would try to answer his relevant questions on his own. He had a strong army of FBI agents and his own confidential informants who were entrenched in every nook and cranny throughout Manhattan. Rivero's informants were of every race, color, and creed, loyal only to themselves. Their main objective was to avoid lifetime sentences for having terrorist ties so they could continue to sell their drugs on the streets, pimp their prostitutes, and stay home with their families.

In Manhattan, a sitting federal grand jury had been selected within two weeks of the Macy's massacre. That investigative body had the power to subpoena anybody, if you knew whom to subpoena, to testify before them under threat of contempt and incarceration. The nighttime security staff at Macy's was scared to death to come in because of possible retaliation for their limited cooperation. Their testimony was not freely given, but they made it clear that on the night before the bombing while Macy's was closed, six black-hooded assailants with AK47s had corralled them and threatened them and their children with death unless they remained silent until after the bombs were placed and detonated.

That's all they knew, and though Rivero suspected that one may have known more and was part of the conspiracy, he had no evidence to justify pursuing that possibility. Rivero knew his city had hot spots for terrorist cells, locales where terrorists could get together to conspire and plan their next act of death and destruction. An anonymous tip, which could have been from a confidential informant who wanted to remain incognito, advised that the Macy's Six had operated out of a terrorist cell in a back alley garage on Grove Street at Sheridan Square, New York. That led to the storming of that site by a cadre of FBI agents with their own semiautomatic weapons drawn and in full gear, accompanied by armored vehicles with tanklike destructive power. The invasion based on that tip discovered no persons whatsoever at the site, but a search of the premises produced plenty of evidence that the Macy's Six had been there at one time. Sketches of Macy's floor plans, which included all entrances and exits, were found in a desk. Bomb-making materials were still on the floor. Fingerprint dusting produced nothing, but the fact they had spent time there was obvious.

Rivero made another discovery at that site that frightened and concerned him, but he kept it under tight wraps. To be specific, that locale had been used prior to the 9/11 attack for the same purposes, which meant that it may have been continuously active since 2001. Photographs of the Twin Towers, White House, and Pentagon were found there and seized. All of them subsequently traced to August 2001. Equally disturbing to Rivero was the discovery of layouts of New York City's mass transit subway lines, with red stars marking both Penn Station and Forty-Second Street. Newspapers headlining the assassination of Osama bin Laden on May 2, 2011, were scattered throughout.

To Rivero, this meant the Macy's bombing was al-Qaeda related and not ISIS (which he never believed anyway), giving him even more reason to be concerned, very concerned. The hooded six were still out there in the United States, probably Manhattan, and who knew what the fuck they were up to.

* * *

Frank Carlucci and Stephanie Jackson sat in the assigned room at the Dauphin County Prison across from their client. The client, still dressed in his orange jumpsuit with "DCP" on the back, waited in silence to learn the purpose of this visit by his lawyers. He did not appear stressed at all, and the rigors of being housed under maximum security at the Dauphin County Prison seemed to have taken no outward toll.

Carlucci and Jackson had done everything he asked them to do, which was absolutely nothing. Judge Joseph James and the United States Attorney's Office were baffled that no pretrial motions had been filed, and when it was set forth in writing that it was not an oversight but rather a directive from their client, there was nothing more to say. Judge James had called everyone to his chambers more than once for status conferences, at which times the defense lawyers continued to reaffirm that nothing was going to be filed and that the defense was prepared to try the case as scheduled.

Carlucci had difficulty disguising his nervousness. "Sir," Carlucci said respectfully, breaking the silence, "The reason we're here is to bring certain developments to your attention that we believe are important for you to know. First of all, we've done everything you've asked and will continue to honor your wishes as long as your wishes are lawful."

Their client acknowledged that he understood.

"We have just received from the government," Carlucci continued after clearing his throat, "two jailhouse confessions. Do you know what a jailhouse confession is?"

The client nodded.

"Ms. Jackson and I feel we can deal with these jailhouse confessions because they come from corrupt sources. There's no guarantee, but we know ways to handle this. Our more serious concern is a lab report that was turned over to us in discovery from Quantico, Virginia. The report indicates that your DNA was on the bomb that blew up State Street." There was noticeable concern in Carlucci's voice as he disclosed this information, and both he and Jackson stared at their client, searching his face intently for a reaction.

There was no reaction.

"Do you want to talk about this?" Carlucci asked, for this DNA discovery would normally have been terrible news for any client.

"Again, I ask you to pay attention," the client said in that all-too-familiar eerie tone. "I appreciate your difficult position and that you came out here to bring me the news. The jailhouse confessions and the DNA report are lies. I'll deal with them on the witness stand when you call me."

"Well," Carlucci said, "Do you at least want to talk about jury selection?"

"Certainly," the client answered and made short work of that inquiry. "Jury selection on our part is going to be very easy . . . We will pick the first twelve."

Their client then stood up and knocked on the door for the guards to come get him, telling them as he departed, "Stay calm."

* * *

The trial in Pennsylvania was days away. All the snow had melted in Downtown Harrisburg, but the brisk March wind coming off the Susquehanna River was a reminder that spring had not yet arrived. The flags at the Capitol were at full mast and flying. It was business as usual on the hill, but precautions were being taken at the federal courthouse for the commencement of the upcoming trial.

The United States Marshal's Office had ramped up the detection machines and scanners at the entrance to the courthouse, which would require everybody to remove their shoes. More personnel in uniform would be brought in to screen all arriving visitors at the entrance. Outside, there would be uniformed and plainclothes officers trained to watch for any suspicious activity. Every floor, including the basement and roof of the federal courthouse, the site of the trial, would be policed.

Though no terrorist group had claimed an "association" with John Doe, no one knew what to expect when he would be brought to the courthouse to be tried. Every measure would be taken to provide him safety as well, since he was being charged for causing the death of thousands, and a parent or spouse grieving for a lost loved one could be lying in wait. This case was to be tried in a court of law, but the competency of the American criminal justice system would be decided in the court of public opinion worldwide; consequently, a public assassination of this defendant was not an option.

The following court order was posted on the Internet, and hard copies were delivered by hand to the United States Attorney's Office on the second floor and to the Federal Public Defender's Office.

<u>ORDER</u>

NOW, this 10th day of March 2016, **IT IS HEREBY ORDERED** that jury selection in the case of <u>United States v. John Doe</u> will begin on **Monday, March 14, 2016,** at the Ronald Reagan Federal Building & U.S. Courthouse, 228 Walnut Street, Harrisburg, PA.

Trial will begin immediately after a jury has been selected.

IT IS FURTHER ORDERED as follows:

1. Cameras and video recorders of any kind (including smartphone cameras and laptop computer/tablet cameras) and audio devices of any kind are PROHIBITED in the courtroom.

2. Taking of photographs and making of video and audio recordings are PROHIBITED in the courthouse.

3. Cellular phones, pagers, smartphones, computers, or other electronic devices are NOT PERMITTED in the courtroom(s).

4. No interviews are permitted inside the courthouse.

5. All spectators, including media representatives, are expected to be seated fifteen (15) minutes before court begins.

6. Courtroom Number 1.

    A. Reserved Seating. Once a jury has been selected, there will be reserved seating for:
        i. Defendants' families and close personal friends.
        ii. Media representatives with credentials.
        iii. The general public on a first-come-first-served basis until seating is full to capacity.

7. All other courtrooms in the Ronald Reagan Federal Building & U.S. Courthouse will not be used for ordinary business. All aforesaid courtrooms will serve as remote locations for the audio and video transmission of the proceedings from Courtroom One. Members of the general public and the media are authorized to access these courtrooms. Courtroom cameras will be fixed on the witness, counsel, and the Court, with no filming of the jury. Exhibits admitted into evidence and published to the jury will not be displayed in these courtrooms.

8. Sketch artist preparing drawings of court proceedings are prohibited from drawing detailed sketches of any member of the jury; however, silhouettes with no distinguishing features may be produced.

9. There will be a media assembly room in the area outside the Clerk's office on the first floor of the courthouse in which the media may gather and transmit by cellular phone, computer, or other electronic devices. Only credentialed members of the media will be permitted to enter this room.

10. Jury Contacts and Security:

   A. Any attempts to contact or interact with jurors to obtain the location of their residences or jobsites, or to otherwise ascertain their identities in any way, are prohibited.

   B. Conversations, interviews, and written communications with prospective jurors before the completion of voir dire, and selected jurors, including alternate jurors, before the Court has discharged the jury at the conclusion of the trial (before a verdict is reached) are prohibited.

   C. After a verdict has been rendered and the Court has discharged the jury, any juror may consent to talk with anyone they choose concerning the case. However, they are not obligated to do so, and there must be no further attempts to speak with jurors who have indicated a desire not to have such discussions.

11. Information regarding these proceedings will be available at http://www.pamd.uscourts.gov. The web page will be updated daily when trial begins.

12. Any violation of any portion of this Order may result in the imposition of contempt sanctions against the violator individually and, if attending in the capacity of an employee or agent, against the employer or principal.

/s/Joseph James
Joseph James
United States District Judge

All precautions were now in place for the trial. It was now time to try the case, but like the calm before any storm, the wait was unsettling.

CHAPTER 18

THE TRIAL

March 14, 2016
Ronald Reagan Federal Courthouse
Harrisburg, Pennsylvania

B EFORE DAYLIGHT, THE media trucks were in place with their mobile towers telescoped skyward. Since there was no room for parking this battalion of vehicles in Harrisburg's center city, operators were directed by uniformed personnel to line up on a cartway down by the Susquehanna River, three blocks away. Portable cameras and photographers were permitted on the steps and sidewalks outside the courthouse as was the phalanx of print media reporters. This First Amendment army would occupy Harrisburg until the verdict was announced, and the best estimate was three to four weeks.

It was overcast and blustery outside, but by 6:45 a.m., a line of people were eagerly waiting to get into the courthouse in hopes of getting the best seats. The doors would not open until 8:00 a.m., and then the line would begin to move ever so slowly because of security. Certain high-profile cases are like theater—this was one of them—and the stage was set.

Courtroom 1 was prewired for the production with a sixty-inch flat screen TV facing the jury box, computer screens for each juror, and computer screens for the lawyers built into the counsel tables, one for the judge, another on the witness stand, and a large one facing the gallery so that viewers would be able to see the exhibits clearly.

The other courtrooms that would accommodate the overflow crowd were also wired for visual and audio reception, but hallways were not for curious observers and would be policed by uniformed personnel to maintain order and discipline.

There would be very little silence until the gavel fell.

"Is counsel ready to select a jury?" Judge James asked the lawyers in his chambers. Waiting in the courtroom were one hundred eighty citizens selected at random throughout the Middle District, from which twelve principal jurors and six alternates would be chosen. They would be instructed to listen to the evidence uninfluenced by anything they may have seen, read, or heard beforehand and render their true verdict. They would also be advised, but only after they were selected, that they would be sequestered. The chosen jurors would be housed and fed at the upscale Hilton Harrisburg until the case was over; in other words, they would not be going home.

"The government is ready," answered Mr. Nelson. Indeed they were, for background checks had been complete on each of the one hundred eighty citizens to make sure there were no ringers. They had hired a forensic jury consulting firm from State College to help identify conviction-oriented characteristics in the cadre of candidates. That firm had already reviewed the questionnaires filled out by the prospective jurors that gave a glimpse into their history: name, address, marital status, children, occupation, political affiliation, and relationships to law enforcement officers or the military.

"The defense is ready," answered Mr. Carlucci. He had not notified the court or the government that they planned to pick the first twelve, nor had they filed with the court any proposed questions for the panel.

"Very well, gentlemen," Judge James stated, "I have granted the defense's request to have their client brought into the courtroom before we begin, that his handcuffs and shackles be removed during court proceedings, and that he be permitted to wear civilian clothes as opposed to prison garb. He is presumed innocent until the government proves otherwise beyond a reasonable doubt, and that's my reason for granting their request. Let's get started."

The jury selection process moved with record speed, even with individual voir dire that is required in a federal death penalty case. Jurors were brought into the courtroom one at a time for questioning. The government had a series of questions prepared by the consulting firm to elicit signs of biases and prejudices, with follow-up questions based on jurors' answers. The defense, consistent with their client's instructions, had no questions and took the first twelve approved by the government. From the panel of one hundred eighty prospective jurors, one hundred ten were removed for cause by the court, after having indicated that they had formed a fixed opinion as to the defendant's guilt, and no amount of evidence was going to change their minds.

The final principal jury consisted of eight men and four women; the alternatives consisted of four women and two men. Their ages ranged from twenty-seven to eighty-one. There were twelve Caucasians, four African Americans, and two Hispanics. Their education levels ranged from high school dropout to a doctoral degree in science. Occupations included educator, administrator, secretary, state employee, farmer, former military, and retiree.

That jury was picked in less than a day, and some of the buzz was that the defense had already thrown their client under the bus.

"Is this jury acceptable to the government?" Judge James asked in open court with the jury in the box.

"This jury is acceptable to the government," Mr. Nelson answered formally.

"Is this jury acceptable to the defense?" Judge James asked, looking at defense counsel and the defendant.

"This jury is acceptable to the defense," Mr. Carlucci answered, standing out of respect.

* * *

The court was adjourned for the day by 6:00 p.m. The jurors were permitted to go home to get their things, driven and escorted by the Federal Marshal's Office. They were advised that they would be hearing opening statements the following morning and that the government would go first, and the defense second, but it was made clear that the defense had the right to defer its opening until after the government rested its case and that no particular significance should be ascribed to that tactic.

At no time did Frank Carlucci give any indication that his instruction from the client was to call him to the witness stand. He gave no hint to the government as to what his defense was going to be. That primary reason for that was because he himself had no idea what his defense was going to be and hadn't a clue about his client's testimony. The only comfort available to defense counsel was knowing this case could not be won. You can only lose a case on the courtroom floor if you have a shot at winning it, and this case did not fall into that category.

Before the court adjourned for the day, the defendant whispered a request to his lawyers. He asked them to call an agent by the name of Yvette Lewis to let her know that he harbored no negativity toward her but did what he did so that she wouldn't get close to him. His lawyers were to assure Agent Lewis that her child was never in harm's way; in fact, quite the contrary. He was hoping to see her in court.

"You are not going to be making an opening statement tomorrow," the defendant told his lawyers at the end of the day. "That's my final decision on that matter."

Frank Carlucci silently nodded and was privately relieved since he had no idea what he would say in an opening anyway.

* * *

Jurors are introduced to a case during the critical opening statements. Lawyers are specially trained to describe persuasively just how the case will unfold from the witness stand. This helps the jury begin to visualize each piece of evidence fitting perfectly with the other until the promised picture emerges, like seeing a scene on a puzzle box that shows you what those tiny pieces inside should look like when all of them are correctly in place. Many trial advocates, professors of law, social psychologists, and forensic jury consultants believe that cases are won and lost in the opening, for once the jury forms an opinion, it is hell to change.

Attorney Sam Nelson was ready to make his first appearance on the world stage. He had rehearsed his opening time and time again, at home with his wife, in the office with his staff, and even in the empty courtroom addressing an empty jury box. He liked working from a podium versus standing free. It was more professorial and less theatrical. Nelson even had his closing ready and his direct examination of certain key witnesses. He had assigned Korsakov the other remaining government witnesses for direct, and Korsakov was to be prepared to do the cross-examination of the defendant. Korsakov was totally satisfied with his role.

Nelson walked to the podium in complete control of the courtroom, and the long-awaited kickoff was about to take place. He had a lot to work with, and the kickoff would go long and far with an aggressive lineup to back up everything he said. His opening, with prior court approval and no objection from the defense, would include dimming the lights and flashing the terrifying scenes of all five catastrophic events and then shocking the jury with the defendant's ominous presence at every one of them.

There would be no doubt in the jury's mind, or the world, that the man standing on the Greek church steps on 9/11 . . . or in the subway on 7/7 in London . . . or in the alcove when Macy's was bombed . . . or on the hill watching the Airbus burn . . . or by the top pillar of Pennsylvania's Capitol observing State Street ablaze . . . was the same man sitting in the defendant's chair twelve feet from the jury box.

Sam Nelson didn't need a jury consultant to tell him that his audience of twelve plus six was horrified at what they were hearing and witnessing.

He and Korsakov had discussed it and concluded that Nelson would hold back on the jailhouse confessions in his opening but not the defendant's DNA on the bomb, which would seal the case on the first day of trial. Nelson's opening presentation went on for two hours and would be documented in the legal archives as exceptionally well done.

Throughout the opening, the gallery and the media picked up on the intense stares the jury aimed at the defendant. The defendant at no time reacted but sat patiently with his hands clasped and resting on the table before him. He was not facing the jury, so Judge James took the opportunity to watch him for any hints as to what he was thinking based on his demeanor.

There were no hints whatsoever.

At the conclusion of Nelson's opening, there would be a fifteen-minute break. At that time, the judge summoned the lawyers up to the sidebar and, with his stenographer in place, continued the creation of a record that is required for every trial in America.

"Mr. Carlucci, do you intend to open at this time?" Judge James asked, with the stenographer continuing her arduous task.

"I do not," Carlucci answered, "I defer."

Nelson and Korsakov said nothing in response, but the dark hole where the defense seemed to be hiding was making them both uncomfortable . . . not that it really mattered.

"When we reconvene, Mr. Nelson," the judge said, standing up to take his break, "You can call your first witness."

* * *

For the next several days, with movie-set timing and choreographic flair, Nelson and Korsakov took turns calling witnesses to revisit, via video footage taken by the media or the government or by poster-size color photos, what Nelson had promised the jury in his opening.

The two planes crashed into the Twin Towers, and with smoke billowing in the skyline, people were running up the streets of Manhattan crying in terror. The responders—NYPD, NYFD, and ambulances with sirens screaming—appeared on the sixty-inch flat screen within minutes.

The London subway on 7/7 was bombed again for the jury, and the volume for the presentation was raised to emphasize the moment when the two-tier bus in London blew up before their very eyes.

The jury experienced the Macy's bombing one more time, and the Airbus burning one more time, and the State Street inferno one more time. The State Street inferno was so close in proximity to the courthouse one could almost imagine a faint smell of smoke in the air.

After that, the poster-size digital color photos of the demonized defendant were exhibited. It showed, while the rest of the world had watched the disasters on TV, he had been there live at every one, whether it was in London or America. Then, as jurors and the rest of the courtroom audience shifted their gaze from the photos to the defendant, all of them, almost simultaneously, realized that the man at defense counsel's table looked exactly as he did thirteen years ago. For him, time appeared to have stood still.

The government then shifted to their current witness list, who would testify to their recollections of the recent past. They had their own corrupt history, but the government always points out that it's the defendant who chooses his friends in a prison environment. The defendant's friends, the government always contends, have a right to be rewarded for coming forward with meaningful information.

The first jailhouse informant was Carl Elliott Sanderson, and he was quite a character. Carl, aged forty-eight, was being held in Dauphin County Prison without bail for child molestation, having forced himself "allegedly" on his ten-year-old stepdaughter, going so far as penile penetration, over a one-year period.

"Mr. Sanderson," Korsakov asked, having laid out his witness's history gingerly, "While you were in Dauphin County Prison awaiting disposition of your case, did you have an opportunity to befriend and talk to the defendant?"

"I did, sir," Carl answered deferentially.

"Tell the jury in your own words about that relationship and what he said to you," Korsakov directed him.

"Well, he was kind of a loner and so was I, so I tried to hang out with him, and we'd sit together at lunch. One day, we were by ourselves at the end of one of those long tables we eat at, and he just said that he hated the fucking government . . . that they're pigs or words to that effect . . . and it was time to get their attention. I'm not sure exactly how he said it, but that's the gist."

"What did you say to him after he told you that?" Korsakov asked.

"I . . . I didn't know what to say . . . I got away from him. He scared me, and I never hooked up with him again," Carl answered.

Carlucci brought out on cross-examination that in exchange for his cooperation, a plea agreement had been reached. The plea agreement read that in exchange for his "truthful cooperation," the charges would be reduced to indecent contact and that he would be released within thirty days. Those plea agreements always have the proviso that the cooperation must be truthful, and in this instance, you can't argue that he didn't have indecent contact.

Korsakov's second inmate witness wasn't much better than the first. Bobby Barnes Burnheiser, aged twenty-one, was in the same prison for a string of nighttime house burglaries, all felonies, and was facing a certain ten years from the judge assigned to his case. In exchange for Bobby's truthful cooperation against the defendant, he would get to appear before a more lenient judge, with a sentence not to exceed eleven and one-half to twenty-three months.

"Tell the jury, Bobby, in your own words, what you overheard the defendant say to Mr. Sanderson in the cafeteria the day they were having lunch together," Korsakov asked.

"I was just taking my empty tray back to clean it off, and I overheard something about 'I hate the government' . . . something about pigs . . . and something about it was time to get the government's attention," he told the jury, making it clear that it was a onetime incident, and that's all he knew.

Carlucci brought out for the jury that Sanderson and Burnheiser were cellmates and that he intended to stress in his closing argument that this alleged world-renowned terrorist—believed to be a mastermind with ISIS—would never hang around with or confide in the likes of Carl and Bobby, two country boys with issues.

The defendant's alleged buddies didn't even know his name.

But Korsakov wasn't finished yet; his best was yet to come. His next witness was not from Dauphin County Prison. His next witness had no baggage. His next witness had no deal to cut with anybody. His next witness was the chief DNA expert and a Michigan State PhD who worked for the esteemed FBI crime lab in Quantico, Virginia, the most reputable in the world. Her name was Dr. Jennifer Janson, and when she walked into the courtroom with her file, dressed in a blue pin-striped business suit and white blouse, hair in a bun, she looked the part.

Korsakov spent forty-five minutes laying out her credentials: science major, an earned PhD from Michigan State, doctoral thesis on DNA, ten-year experience at the federal crime unit in Quantico working with DNA, and had testified over two hundred times in thirty-four states as a blood and DNA expert. In this case, she had a vial with her of the defendant's blood and remnants of the bomb taken from a basement on State Street that was linked to that terrorist act.

"In my opinion, beyond reasonable scientific certainty, the defendant's DNA was on the remnants of the bomb provided, which contained microscopic traces of blood." She looked directly at the jury as she testified, which is what professional experts are taught to do. Her presentation was technical but supported with clarifying charts on easels and which contained overwhelming evidence of the defendant's guilt.

"What are the statistical odds," Korsakov asked her, knowing what her answer was going to be and knowing this was the stake in the heart of this modern-day Dracula, "that your DNA findings from these traces of blood on the bomb remnants could be someone else's?"

"The Bureau of Statistics that is the Bible of our industry puts it at ten million to one," she answered.

Upon hearing this stunning conclusion, Korsakov whispered to Nelson, "Game over."

CHAPTER 19

THE LONE WOLF

THE GOVERNMENT RESTED its case before noon on Saturday, March 26, and though it was early in the day, the court adjourned the proceedings until Monday morning at nine. This was the second six-day week in a row, but the good news was that the case was moving along, and everyone's interest was intense. Judge James was convinced there would be a verdict by early next week, possibly Monday if the defense presented no evidence. He was also convinced the case was over for John Doe even without the jailhouse informants' testimony and without the DNA "stake." Two poster-size photos of the defendant placed at two different terrorist-generated tragedies—nothing more—would be enough for any jury to convict beyond a reasonable doubt.

Judge James had no idea what Carlucci had in mind now that the ball was in his court.

Media pundits and talk show hosts had no idea what Carlucci was going to do either. Open? Rest? Jump out the window?

Most important, Carlucci had no idea what Carlucci was going to do.

Nobody did.

Except John Doe; at least he said he did. Before he was handcuffed and shackled and taken to DCP for the weekend, he told his two lawyers, "Do not make the deferred opening argument. Just call me to the witness stand, and I'll take it from there." That parting instruction by the client was totally fine with Carlucci—totally, totally,

totally—because he honestly had no clue what to say that would have any authority.

The court wanted a brief conference in chambers before breaking for the weekend. Judge James wanted to get some idea about when he would be charging the jury on the law. This would require an estimate from Carlucci on how long his case was going to take. The lawyers could also discuss the judge's points for charge on mass murder and terrorism, although the charges were pretty straightforward. Killing people with bombs and fires and crashing planes was mass murder, pretty easy to understand.

Sam Nelson and Fran Korsakov were present in chambers for the government.

Frank Carlucci and Ms. Jackson were present in chambers for the Defendant.

The court stenographer was in the ready position, seated beside the judge's mahogany desk.

"How long is your opening going to take, Frank?" Judge James asked. "I'm not going to restrict your time, but if you could give me a rough idea, it would be helpful."

"Your Honor, there's not going to be a deferred opening," Carlucci answered unapologetically.

Nelson and Korsakov looked at each other, startled.

"Are you going to be calling any witnesses?" the judge asked.

"No," Carlucci answered.

"Are you going to go directly into your closing argument?" Judge James asked, thinking this case was really wrapping up fast.

"No," Carlucci answered, and after a moment of stunned silence by everyone else in the room, the defense lawyer dropped another bomb for the government to deal with. "My client will be taking the stand first thing Monday morning. He is waiving his right to remain silent. He has authorized me to bring this decision to the attention of the court and the government at this conference."

It really was a bomb, but no one in that room knew where it would be coming from or where it would be aimed, including Carlucci, who promised to launch it.

* * *

WILLIAM C. COSTOPOULOS

Word got out fast and spread quickly. The banner headline in the *New York Times* Sunday edition was John Doe Will Testify, in the *Washington Post* Terrorist to Take Stand, and in the *Philadelphia Inquirer* Answers Are Coming.

By Monday morning, the world knew the "man with no name" would be taking the stand. No one had any idea as to what he was going to say, which stirred everyone's curiosity. The dwindling attendance over the past two weeks, though it didn't dwindle much, was back to an overflow crowd in the galleries. There would be VIPs in the preferred seating section who were there for the first time. Liam Spokane, director of counterintelligence, would be in the first row. Seated beside him would be Agent George Yoder; beside Yoder would be Agent Yvette Lewis, along with John Rivero, the United States attorney from New York. The FBI liaison with Russia was asked to be present and would be accompanied by Putin's FSB counterpart. This could be a break for all agencies involved.

* * *

The walls of the Federal Building pulsated with expectancy as everyone made their way into the courtroom. The media had given top billing to John Doe's appearance on the witness stand, and the second act of this theater performance promised to be a thriller. The air in courtroom 1 was thick with excitement and tension. The jury was wide awake, knowing they had a major role to play in this historic moment.

"May it please the court," Carlucci said, at exactly 9:00 a.m. "The defense calls the defendant to the witness stand." Carlucci didn't say it with any sense of drama, but what he said was pretty dramatic.

The man . . . known as John Doe . . . the defendant himself . . . got out of his chair with absolute calm and fired his first shot at the government; even before taking the witness stand, he challenged the court by refusing to raise his right hand or swear on the Bible. He wasn't "affirming" anything. He just took his seat on the witness stand and made himself comfortable.

No one, not the government or the court, made an issue of his actions because maybe he just wasn't all there.

"Sir," Carlucci began with his direct examination, standing with his hands on the podium facing his client, "Would you please state your name for the record?"

"No," answered his client.

And nobody knew what to do, but after what seemed an eternity, Judge James leaned toward the defendant with both courtesy and caution.

Until the judge made the effort to address this awkward moment, Nelson and Korsakov stood paralyzed. Carlucci's heart practically flatlined. The gallery was glad they were where they were and not directly in the game.

"Sir," Judge James said, "You've elected to waive your right to remain silent by taking the witness stand. In our system of justice, having waived that right, you just can't pick and choose what questions you want to answer. I will allow you to confer with your counsel and thereafter decide whether you still want to testify. Do you understand your options?"

Everybody in the courtroom held their breath.

"Please pay attention to me, Your Honor," the defendant said respectfully, but the words "pay attention" went through Carlucci like a knife, for he had heard them before, more than once, and it always preceded a hell of a follow-up . . . and Carlucci was not to be disappointed.

The defendant leaned toward the judge, just as the judge had done to him, not in a threatening way but in a polite one, and stated his position about his options and rules. "I was at those five sites of terror where thousands of people were slaughtered . . . I watched each event unfold from beginning to end . . . I know who did what, and how, and why . . . I had a very important role that I'm willing to tell this jury about . . . and you too, Your Honor. You might be interested in hearing this . . . I know the government will be."

The defendant continued with his unsolicited testimony, not only recorded by the stenographer but also was being electronically transmitted throughout the world. The world that really mattered at this moment, however, was in the jury box, consisting of those four women, eight men, and six alternates, and they sent the unspoken message to Judge James that they were very interested in what the defendant had to say . . . And their message was quite clear.

"Now," he continued, still respectful but with a trace of boldness, "If you want answers to those questions—who was responsible for those terrorist acts and what my role was—*you* have two options, not I. Option 1 is to allow me to answer them, but I have every intention of picking and choosing which questions to answer from those I might be asked. Option 2 is to remove me from the witness stand and have this jury put me to death. I am personally content with either decision."

The judge could not fathom such audacity, and he could feel his authority being challenged, but the promise to tell the world what it wanted to know could not be summarily dismissed. Judge Joseph James called for an immediate meeting in chambers, told the jury that they would be excused for a short recess, directed the stenographer to set up in his chambers, and then disappeared.

Nelson and Korsakov were in a state of shock. Carlucci and Jackson, even with their history involving their client, were in a similar condition. John Rivero passed a note to Nelson that he wanted to participate in this conference in chambers and so did Liam Spokane. Frankly, everyone in the courtroom would have liked to do the same.

Judge James granted Rivero's request since he was the sitting United States attorney in New York whose case was at issue. He denied the request of Liam Spokane.

Everybody in chambers had an agenda, and the record transcribed would be read in law schools for years to come.

"Mr. Carlucci," Judge James began, a little edgy and noticeably angry, "Did you know this was coming?"

"No, Your Honor," he answered respectfully and added, "I don't even know his name."

"Did your client undergo a psychiatric exam? I signed the petition authorizing payment for such an expert. Did you go through with that?" the judge asked, again in an irritated tone.

"I did, Your Honor," Carlucci answered, and with that, he reached into his file and produced for the court and the government the written report prepared by Dr. Lisa Schneider, which read in relevant part as follows:

> Having examined one John Doe at the Dauphin
> County Prison at the request of Attorneys Carlucci and
> Jackson to determine whether this patient/defendant

was competent to stand trial and whether this patient/ defendant was potentially criminally insane, it is the opinion of this author, beyond reasonable medical and psychiatric certainty, that John Doe is competent to stand trial. He certainly understands the nature of the proceedings and is in a position to assist counsel in the process. There is no indication that he is criminally insane, said standard set forth in the landmark case of *McNaughton*. This opinion was without the availability of any previous mental health records, medical reports, other institutional reports, or personal history, and I was advised that none were available.

The judge read the psychiatric report prepared by Dr. Lisa Schneider for the stenographer to transcribe.

"What's the government's position?" Judge James asked looking directly at U.S. Attorney Nelson.

"May I speak?" John Rivero asked, before Nelson could respond.

"Of course," Judge James said, recognizing John Rivero and his status.

"Thank you, Your Honor," Rivero replied. "For the record, my name is John Rivero, and I am the sitting United States attorney for the New York Southern District. That district includes most of New York City, including Manhattan. On November 28, 2014, Macy's Department Store was bombed and burned. The details of this terrorist act have been testified to in this courtroom. The presence of the defendant on that day has been established by the government in this courtroom, and indeed, the defendant has done so as well. Not only did he confirm his presence but he also announced that he was willing to testify to his role, who was involved, how it was brought about, and even why. I would ask that he be permitted to answer these important questions whether he has mental health issues or not or even if he wants to pick and choose his questions. My reasons should be obvious. I have an ongoing investigation, and I will know if this individual is legitimate or not."

"Mr. Nelson?" The judge was asking for his position, on the record, having understood Rivero's position completely.

"Your Honor," Nelson began, "I understand Mr. Rivero's position, and I too have an interest in this defendant's professed knowledge that he's now willing to share. I don't know what we're getting into, and I have a lot of concerns about any defendant picking and choosing his questions, but I agree with Mr. Rivero. My position for the record is to meet the defendant's demands and let him testify."

"Mr. Carlucci?" Judge James asked.

"I don't know anything, Your Honor," Carlucci answered. "I join in the government's motion."

"Okay, gentlemen," Judge James said, concerned about the dignity and decorum of the upcoming proceedings, "I'll let him testify, and we'll see what happens."

While the conference was going on in chambers, a proceeding that took an hour, the defendant was permitted to remain in the courtroom under the careful watch of United States marshals. No one in the gallery moved, not even to take a break, because they didn't want to lose their seats. The tipstaff's announcement that the court proceedings were about to resume was a welcome announcement. The "man with no name" resumed the witness stand, knowing he would have his way.

Mr. Carlucci went back to the podium without his prepared notes, which would have been worthless.

"Sir," Mr. Carlucci began for the second time, "Where do you normally live?"

"I live in hell," the defendant answered matter-of-factly.

Carlucci gulped at the answer, but he was an experienced lawyer, and that answer needed clarification. "Sir," Carlucci continued, "I know that the conditions you've have been under in confinement have been very restrictive, very unpleasant, maybe even punitive, but I wasn't referring to your present environment. My question refers to your living arrangements prior to your apprehension."

"I wasn't referring to my present environment, Mr. Carlucci," his client responded. "I was referring to where I lived prior to my apprehension . . . I live in hell as opposed to heaven."

With that answer, Judge James called an immediate sidebar, while the witness remained where he was. Judge James just wanted reaffirmation on the record that the government and defense counsel wished for this to play out. Judge James got his reaffirmation.

Carlucci had no idea what his next question should be, so throwing caution to the winds, he asked what would normally be a typical question. "What do you do for a living, sir?"

That having been asked, which was the one for which the defendant had been waiting, caused the defendant to shift his position on the witness stand and face the jury, which is what professional witnesses do. The jury couldn't even look at him and would soon have even more reason not to.

"My mission is to assess evil, and if my assessment of evil reaches a certain level of heinous wrongdoing, then I am to follow up by taking sinners who meet or exceed that monstrous standard to hell on an expedited basis. I am not the main man . . . that's Satan . . . but I am of high rank. I speak and act on his behalf, and I am here on his behalf."

The stenographer and the scribes for the media were having a hard time writing this down for no one was ready for what they were hearing; it was frighteningly surreal. The judge, the government, defense counsel, and the gallery all braced themselves as the witness spoke to them from the world he knew best . . . and the one his audience feared most. The defendant did not pause for a moment in his presentation because he had much more to say.

"You see," he continued, "Heaven is real . . . and because heaven is real, so is hell . . . I believe your good judge in this courtroom, the Honorable Joseph James, would agree with that."

With that piece of testimony, he gave Judge James, who had been staring at him, unblinking, a respectful glance . . . and the witness knew he had hit a nerve.

"Ladies and gentlemen," this professed agent of the devil continued, "When evil rises to the level you've been experiencing on this earth, there is no reason for us to wait in hell for those souls. There is no amount of prayer that will bring them redemption . . . and no reason to let them continue on this earth and bring harm to more innocent people. In such situations, God is in concurrence with a program to expedite our taking of their souls. That having been said, we've been very busy. The level of terrorist evil this world is engaging in—9/11, 7/7, the Macy's bombing, the State Street fire, the Russian Airbus catastrophe, massacres in elementary schools and movie theaters, I could go on and on—is being handled. In summation, I was at those five sites as an agent of the devil. I assessed the level of evil, expedited the process for many of the perpetrators, and I now have their souls in hell."

"Your Honor," the professed agent from hell said, shifting in the witness stand to look at Judge James, "I am now prepared to hear other questions I promised to answer."

"Sir," Judge James said to the witness respectfully, "It is not my province in our system of justice to question you. I certainly have a wide range of authority, but I will leave the questions to counsel."

"I understand," the defendant replied.

"Mr. Carlucci," the judge said, signaling defense counsel to follow up on his client's proffer.

Carlucci now had some idea of where he was going to go with his direct examination now that the foundation had been laid by his client. He was actually a bit excited for the first time since he was assigned this case. "Sir, you testified earlier that you could shed some light on who did what, and how, and why. What can you tell us about 9/11?"

"Plenty," his client responded and continued with his articulate presentation.

"What happened in Manhattan on 9/11 rose to the level of unspeakable tragedy, and I was there to witness it. The American investigation and outrage was justified and the judgment that al-Qaeda was responsible in the planning and execution correct. And it was also correct that Osama bin Laden was the mastermind. I didn't have to do anything to take the souls of the terrorist pilots who took control of the planes because they took their own lives. We received their souls the following morning. We now have Osama bin Laden's. There were eight others we took, who were unknown to the United States government even though they were working out of a garage in an alley behind Grove Street, at Sheridan Square in New York City."

With that, John Rivero was incredulous, for his boys having raided that garage gave authority to the testimony. Rivero wasn't convinced yet that the defendant wasn't part of the 9/11 conspiracy as a human being, nor was he persuaded that this guy was from hell, not at all. Rivero sent a note to Carlucci asking him to request the names of the eight souls taken.

"Sir," Carlucci began, having read the note, "What are the names of the eight you took who were operating out of that garage?"

"I'm not answering that question," the client said. "That's one of the questions I refuse to answer, and here's my reason. I'm not here to do the work of criminal prosecutors in any country. Many of these souls we have taken have innocent family members still living on this earth, and such disclosure would bring them immediate harm. God, in his infinite wisdom, has agreed to this expedited soul-taking, but nondisclosure regarding identification of the souls taken was one of his conditions."

Carlucci looked back at Rivero and shrugged his shoulders. Rivero was now convinced more than ever that this guy was a fraud.

"What can you tell me about the July 7, 2007, bombing in London?" Carlucci asked.

"Those bombers," his client answered, "were of British descent . . . They were a splinter group of al-Qaeda, but Osama bin Laden had nothing to do with it. The suicide bombers in the subway and double-decker bus went straight to hell the following morning. There were ten other British extremists that I determined should be taken . . . and they are now burning in hell with their coconspirators. And again, the names of those other ten will not be disclosed for the reason previously given."

Liam Spokane and Agent Yoder were very suspicious about all this. Agent Yvette Lewis was willing to wait with her verdict, for some of his testimony was consistent with what she learned in her religion courses at Bucknell. His message to her as delivered by Carlucci was beginning to make sense, but she needed to hear more.

AUSA Fran Korsakov was furiously taking notes on yellow pads, preparing for a killer cross-examination.

"What can you tell us about the Airbus crash?" Carlucci asked.

"I can tell you this," the witness replied. "ISIS had absolutely nothing to do with that catastrophe. Vladimir Putin is correct and has been all along. Neither did al-Qaeda, and again, Vladimir Putin was correct when he surmised that Manhattan was not the target. That calamity was brought about because of Putin's insurgents in Ukraine, who caused the deaths of many innocent people, including small children. That Airbus was hotwired by three Eastern Orthodox Christians who had the schooling required for such a sophisticated hacking job. It was an act of retaliation, but having been to the site of the crash, I have already determined that it was time to take those three souls and have done so. Putin has a list of six. On that list are three innocents, and I have the other three. No FSB in the world is going to find them. Soon some of Putin's FSB boys will be joining us in hell in the very near future."

The FSB's agent in the courtroom was sweating profusely as the testimony continued because the defendant clearly knew the status of their investigation, and his testimony had just confirmed how they operated. *Maybe*, the FSB agent thought, *It's time to get into another line of work.*

Carlucci had two more attacks to ask about—Macy's and State Street—and because no one was objecting to his client's narratives, he kept going with the momentum he had generated. Carlucci was starting to like his client by now and mused to himself that liking a professed agent of Satan might not be a good idea.

Judge James gave no indication that he was interested in a break.

Fran Korsakov was still frantically taking notes preparing for his cross-examination.

The jury was looking a little frightened.

"Sir," Carlucci asked. "What can you tell us about the Macy's Department Store bombing and burning on November 28, 2014?"

"That bombing," the witness answered on cue, "was planned and carried out by Osama bin Laden's loyalists here in America. That act of terrorism on November 28 at Macy's was in retaliation for the killing of Osama bin Laden by America's Navy Seals on May 2, 2011, shortly after 1:00 a.m. Pakistani time. The killing of their founder and leader was carried out in a CIA-led operation. Al-Qaeda thereafter confirmed his death on May 6, 2011, and posted their vow to avenge the killing on militant websites.

"That was the motive for the bombing.

"It was carried out by six al-Qaeda operatives who entered Macy's Department Store at night. All were hooded and unidentifiable, all carrying semiautomatic weapons. Once in the store, they corralled the night-shift security guards and threatened them, promising to execute their children if any of the guards alerted anyone before the detonation. None of those guards were involved as may have been suspected by some authorities.

"These six Islamic terrorists," the witness continued, who appeared to be gaining credibility with each spoken word, "like the 9/11 contingency in America, planned and implemented their attack on Macy's out of the same garage in an alley on Sheridan Square, New

York. That garage was their cell and camp in the heart of New York City for almost fifteen years."

Rivero could not bring himself to believe that this fucking nut who professed to be an agent of Satan was legitimate. On the other hand, the witness knew a lot, in fact, almost everything in Rivero's file. Rivero's only explanation to himself was that the witness himself could be the mastermind of everything he was telling this jury.

To Rivero, placing blame for the Airbus crash on three Eastern Orthodox extremists out of Ukraine had to be a red herring. This witness could not have been the mastermind of several totally unrelated terrorist organizations. Yet why did that plane miss Manhattan and crash instead in an unpopulated area in New Jersey? It all just didn't make sense.

"I have taken the souls of those six Islamic terrorists who entered Macy's, and for that reason, United States Attorney Rivero will never find them . . . They belong to me." Then looking directly at Rivero, the witness added, "The resources of the United States attorney for the Southern District would be better spent looking for a different cell that is active at this time and located on West Eighty-First Street. The chatter will be his paper trail, though he must move quickly now that I've testified."

Now Rivero didn't know what the fuck to think, but if anything of a terrorist nature originated out of West Eighty-First Street, his career was over.

The dead silence in the courtroom was intense.

The witness seemed unfazed by the gravity of his testimony.

"And the State Street burning?" Carlucci asked.

"The State Street burning . . . and bombing . . . here in Harrisburg on February 9, 2015, was the deed of a lone wolf. It's exactly what 'Jihadi John' promised . . . whose soul I have by the way. That calamity was brought about by an American citizen from Dauphin County who resided in an apartment on State Street. He had been radicalized by ISIS . . . He was given the formula for the bomb over the Internet, along with a makeshift gas pump. That lone wolf had unfettered access to the basement of his apartment building, so he was able to tunnel through the other basements and make history. His motive was hatred of your government and law enforcement.

WILLIAM C. COSTOPOULOS

"Just as I did," the witness continued, "He watched State Street burn as he hid behind a pillar on the Capitol steps. I assessed his evil at such a high level that I took him that night . . . He's gone. . . and no further investigation is needed here on earth."

With that, the witness stopped talking and waited calmly for any other questions.

There would be none from Carlucci because his direct examination was done.

The time was 6:30 p.m. Judge James adjourned the court until the following morning, for it had been a very long day for everyone and for the sitting judge in particular. He instructed the jury that the trial would continue at nine the following morning, that they were not to discuss the case between themselves, and that the government would be cross-examining the defendant.

Once the jury left the courtroom, three United States marshals approached the defendant to handcuff and shackle him for transport. They just did it with a little more respect this time.

CHAPTER 20

SOUL WITNESS

B Y EARLY MORNING, the headlines had alerted every nation. The *New York Times* headline was SATAN ON THE STAND, the *Washington Post* headline stated SATAN IS HERE, and the *Philadelphia Inquirer* headline spelled out HELL IN THE COURTROOM. In Europe and Russia and Asia, every headline had the word *Diabalos*.

The television networks recruited priests of every denomination, rabbis, imams, spiritual healers, professors of religion, and deans of theological schools. These experts and pundits had center stage on a topic that had been given very little attention for centuries. The hard questions for these educated guests, many of whom wore the collar, went to the core of John Doe's testimony.

Is it possible that he's a true representative of Satan?

Is his testimony consistent with the Bible?

Is his testimony consistent with the Koran?

Is heaven for real?

Is hell for real?

The world watched these interviews nonstop, and citizens of all nations weighed in on the Internet. There were bloggers. There was Twitter and Facebook. Websites received millions of hits from every continent. From the e-mails, it seemed that no one in the world had slept that night.

There were as many doubters as there were believers. Late night comedians had their jokes reviewed by the networks because this subject was much too sensitive to take any chances.

AUSA Fran Korsakov intended to expose this lying son of a bitch for what he was. Fran was convinced that the defendant knew what he knew because he masterminded it all. He was also convinced that Satan was highly educated but believed that cross-examination is "the great engine of truth," and Korsakov intended to run over him with his train.

At 9:00 a.m. on March 29, 2016, the whistle blew as that train pulled into the station, and Korsakov was ready.

"Sir," he began, his tone far from cordial, "my name is Assistant United States Attorney Fran Korsakov, and I represent the United States government. I'll be doing the cross-examination, and if I ask you anything that you don't understand, please let me know."

"I know who you are," the defendant answered, and many in the courtroom smiled, hoping it was a joke.

Korsakov resented this defendant already, not that he didn't before.

"Is it your testimony that you are Satan, and you live in a house in hell?" Korsakov asked mockingly.

"I am an agent of Satan . . . I am not Satan . . . and there are no houses in hell . . . That's my testimony," the defendant answered, correcting Korsakov.

"Why didn't you stop these evil terrorists before they killed over three thousand people in New York on 9/11 . . . before they bombed London . . . before they massacred the innocent people at Macy's . . . on the Airbus . . . on State Street? Why did you wait until after the killing of all these innocent people?" Korsakov asked the question he'd crafted specifically to emphasize his point.

"The reason, counselor, is this . . ." The Defendant seemed in total control even before he responded. "When God made man . . . and there is a God . . . he gave him free will. God's entire creation was premised on free will, and it was man's choice to be either good or bad. God was not going to interfere with his grand scheme of creating man after his own likeness by denying him free will.

You may recall that he did not interfere when a prophet by the name of Jesus Christ was hung on a cross and executed. He certainly could have. My job description doesn't allow me to interfere with man's free will, only to assess the degree of evil after the fact. Then and only then can I act."

A hush fell over the courtroom after *that* response.

And the experts and the pundits who were now being interviewed live as the defendant's testimony streamed across the screen were prolific with their approvals and suspicions.

"Well, sir, Mr. Agent of Satan, how do you take these souls from this earth? Do you shoot them? Stab them? Set them on fire maybe?" Korsakov asked, his voice bitter with sarcasm.

"That's a question I'm not going to answer. I can assure you that how I take them varies from case to case, but the result is always the same. The result is that they no longer walk the face of this earth. They're in hell where there are no houses," the witness answered quietly.

Sam Nelson, who was at the podium asking for a recess, handed Korsakov a note. Sam did not like the way things were going. He felt that Korsakov's tone was counterproductive and that this witness's answers were too damaging to the government's case. But Korsakov would have none of it and kept going.

Korsakov continued confronting the witness. "Where do you draw the line, sir . . . Uh, let me rephrase the question." After a pause, he asked again, "You testified that you assess evil and that once you determine it to have reached a certain degree of egregiousness, your job is to expedite the taking . . . Is there a formula for that assessment?" Korsakov asked.

The witness nodded his head yes and then gave the following response: "God is a merciful God . . . but he made it clear that we are permitted to expedite the taking only when no amount of redemption, or reparation, or prayer, or confession will do any good. These terrorist acts that I witnessed were easy to judge.

"For your personal guidance, counselor," the witness continued, now facing Korsakov eye to eye, "You may want to review the Ten Commandments . . . and note that adultery is on that list, for it causes the greatest injury to family bonds."

And with that answer and explanation, the witness waited for the next question.

Korsakov got off that line of questioning very quickly. Nelson was beside himself, for he knew all about Korsakov's personal life—the secretary, the pending divorce, the estranged children. It wasn't only the metaphoric lethal blow inflicted on Korsakov by the witness that rattled him; it was Nelson's obsession to find out how the witness knew about all that shit.

For those people in the courtroom who knew Korsakov and acknowledged him as the consummate trial lawyer whose finest skill was cross-examination, it was obvious that he was getting pummeled.

Korsakov knew it too and went for the defendant's jugular.

"The government has presented testimony that your DNA was on the bomb that killed eleven apartment dwellers in cold blood, with fifteen others being admitted to Baltimore's intensive care unit. You remember the incident because you were watching it from the Capitol steps. How did your DNA get on the bomb, Mr. Agent of Satan?" Korsakov asked and couldn't wait for this cocky son of a bitch to answer that one.

Everyone in the courtroom was anxious to hear the defendant's answer.

Especially the jury.

And the judge.

"Two weeks before that expert report was prepared," the defendant began his explanation, "You, Mr. Korsakov, without saying one word to your boss, Attorney Nelson, went to Quantico, Virginia, for a private meeting with Dr. Jennifer Janson. At that meeting, you told her that the government could not afford to lose this case and that it would be helpful if my DNA were to be discovered on that bomb.

"I know you were nuanced in your wording, but Janson got the message and gave you what you wanted. What you—"

"Objection, Your Honor!" Korsakov screamed, "The witness is speculating!"

Judge James did not rule on the objection and simply told Korsakov, "Let him finish his answer."

"Mr. Korsakov, what you did was wrong. What Janson did to accommodate you was evil. You both knew this was a death penalty case. America prides itself on its system of justice, and the foundation of that system is due process. Due process means that fundamental fairness is afforded an accused individual . . . and what you and Janson did is reprehensible. In fact, in a death penalty case, it's a form of murder.

"Your two jailhouse confessions," the defendant said, continuing without being asked, "were intended to be nails in the coffin, weren't they? I know they were, you know they were, and I hold you more responsible for that disgraceful scheme than your perjurious witnesses."

"Objection, Your Honor!" Korsakov shouted, hoping to stop this debacle.

"Are you finished?" the judge asked the defendant.

"No, Your Honor," answered the witness.

"I will let you finish," the judge ruled.

"You know, counselor," the witness said, "You are a very gifted man and trial lawyer. God gave you that gift. His strategy is to give certain blessings and gifts to certain people and not others . . . in music, in the arts, in medicine, and in law . . . He gave you that gift and free will . . . You could have used that gift to benefit society and your fellow man, but your hubris has taken you down. Now, Your Honor, I'm finished."

"Any further questions, Mr. Korsakov?" the judge asked.

"No, Your Honor," Korsakov answered. "The witness is too hostile."

"That will be for the jury to decide," the judge concluded.

"Any other witnesses, Mr. Carlucci?" the judge asked.

"No, Your Honor. The defense rests," Carlucci answered.

The government had no rebuttal, and the case of *United States v. John Doe* ended with the defendant's final testimony. The defense waived its closing. Sam Nelson, on behalf of the United States government, abbreviated his and asked the jury to take a close look at the exhibits that would accompany them to the jury room. Nelson reminded the jury that the defendant had a stake in the outcome of these proceedings and to weigh the credibility of his testimony with that in mind.

The court's charge was right out of the book.

At that juncture, the jury was retired for the night, and their deliberations would begin the following morning, March 30, continuing until a verdict was reached.

The court adjourned.

CHAPTER 21

THE WAIT

WAITING FOR A jury verdict in any case is stressful certainly for a defendant when his life is in their hands but also for the lawyers who had put it all on the line.

Waiting for a jury verdict in the case of *United States v. John Doe*—with the world waiting and watching—created immense stress for everyone. Plus, the wait for this verdict was going to last for seven days and nights, the same amount of time it took to create heaven and earth, according to Genesis.

In the meantime, there was much to talk about, and emotions ranged all the way from rage to anxiety to wide-eyed wonder. The talk Sam Nelson was seeking to have in his office at 8:00 a.m. on the first day of deliberations was to include all the aforementioned feelings and then some. Korsakov wasn't sure about what was so important that it had to be first thing in the morning . . . but he had a pretty good idea.

Nelson lost a lot of sleep after the defense rested, tossing and turning from worry. The trial had taken a serious toll on him; his nerves were shot, and both his wife and his office staff had noticed the dark circles under his eyes. He avoided restaurants and had relegated himself to eating junk food and snacks in his office. After all, the paparazzi were everywhere.

A late night call from Attorney General Johnson didn't help either. She told him she had seen the evening news from home and then abruptly hung up after announcing that she expected some answers by noon.

Fran Korsakov made sure he was sitting across from his boss's desk at precisely the appointed hour. He knew not to be late by the tone Sam used after the jury went out when he grumbled, "We've got some things to talk about, Fran, like tomorrow at 8:00 a.m." Fran was hoping that Nelson's negativity wasn't about his secret visit to Quantico without telling him . . . but it was.

"You went to Quantico to meet with a DNA expert, and you never told me," Nelson started, without beating around the bush. "Do you know how embarrassing it was for me to learn it from the defendant? Do you have any fucking idea how humiliating that was? I even got a call late last night from the attorney general herself wanting to know what *that* was about. She wants me to call her by noon about it, and so I'm looking for an answer."

It was Fran's worst nightmare, but he had to wake up and deal with it.

"Come on, Sam. Calm down," Fran answered, trying to de-escalate the situation. "I've been with you for eighteen years, and you know I didn't do anything wrong, if that's what you're suggesting. You were busy. You've always given me free reign, and I didn't think anything of it."

"I wasn't that fucking busy," Sam retorted. "I can tell you that Johnson said agents from her office were going to interview Janson. It's probably going on right now, and she better cover your ass on why your meeting was so . . . so private."

Fran said nothing in response and watched his boss crush his third cigarette into the ashtray; Nelson was up to two packs a day and was coughing a lot.

"Do you have any idea, Fran, because I sure as hell don't," Nelson continued with his own cross-examination, "how that defendant who was out of control on the witness stand knew about that meeting?"

"He honestly knew a lot of stuff that surprised me, Sam, and my guess is there's a leak in her office, and Carlucci prepped him," Fran answered, hoping his answer was correct.

"Bullshit" was all Sam had to say and ended the conversation on that note.

* * *

WILLIAM C. COSTOPOULOS

While waiting for the jury to deliberate and return its verdict, there was much to do.

Early morning on the first day, Joe Rivero dispatched a clandestine search team to comb the area of West Eighty-First Street in case, just in case, there was an existing terrorist cell consistent with the agent from hell's claims. He was bemused by the defendant's knowledge of what Rivero knew to be true, but he wasn't convinced that this guy was from another world. In Rivero's mind, the only other world that this defendant was from was the world of terror and deceit and lies. The defendant's knowledge would be consistent with a mastermind who knew it all, and the reference to an existing cell on West Eighty-First Street was a media stunt. He was hoping this covert search team would expose the defendant for what he was—a fucking liar.

Liam Spokane was in agreement with Rivero but not with the same certainty.

Spokane, Yoder, and Lewis were staying at Harrisburg's Crowne Plaza and planned on staying there until the verdict. A lot of the out-of-towners, including many government witnesses, were also staying at the Crowne Plaza because the Hilton was home to the jury and therefore off-limits.

On the first day of deliberations, the three of them—Spokane, Yoder, and Lewis—were having breakfast in a private corner of their hotel. Hot coffee was the first order of business, and then they helped themselves to a buffet of eggs, bacon or ham, home fries, toast or bagels, and pastries. They had sat through the entirety of the defendant's testimony, and there was much to analyze.

"I wasn't ready for that defense," Spokane said, getting the conversation started.

"Neither was I," replied Yoder.

Yvette Lewis nodded in agreement, but it wasn't a definitive response.

They all decided that the jailhouse informants' testimony appeared ridiculous and felt that it may have actually compromised the credibility of the government's case. They granted that there was no way this mysterious man, who had refused to speak to anyone, at any time, for any reason, would confess out of the blue to Carl Sanderson, a pedophile, and coincidently be overheard by a street burglar . . . A situation like that simply doesn't happen.

"It not only didn't happen," Yvette finally chimed in, "The whole thing also sounded absurd."

"What about Korsakov meeting with the DNA expert and not telling Nelson?" Spokane asked.

"That was very embarrassing to Nelson, I can tell you that," Yoder said. "But I was more intrigued by the defendant knowing about it . . . Do we even know that Korsakov had that meeting?" Yoder asked.

"We know Korsakov didn't challenge it," Yvette answered, "And with or without that meeting, I'm awfully suspicious about that expert."

The comment by Yvette triggered a spirited discussion, for to suggest that a government agent from Quantico had planted DNA in a death penalty case was hard for Spokane to comprehend. Not so for Yoder and even less for Lewis. She had seen it before and was pretty sure Janson's name had come up on a previous case despite the report in Lewis's computer data that had cleared her. Yoder and Lewis agreed that whoever this defendant was, he was too important to be handling homemade explosives and would never have left a blood trail.

"Yvette," Spokane asked, looking her straight in the eye, "You're not buying into this agent from hell shit, are you?"

"No," she answered, but her voice was tinged with uncertainty. "How did he know about my five-year-old son?" she asked, and nobody had an answer for her.

* * *

By the third day of deliberations, Judge James was doing a lot of thinking in his chambers. He had to be in his chambers at all times during deliberations just in case the jury had a question and certainly for the taking of the verdict. He was a learned man and a profound jurist and had read the classics and works of the great philosophers. Being a religious man, he had also studied the Old and New Testaments. This defendant, whoever he was, was a real test of his faith, and Judge James was troubled.

The Catholic priest who presided over his church on State Street was a friend of many years, one of a very few. They were almost the same age, seventy-four, and Judge James liked and respected him a lot. An Irishman to the core, the priest's name was Fr. Michael O'Malley, and he was the dean of St. Patrick's Cathedral. Just to kill time and indulge in some intellectualizing while waiting for the verdict or a question, Judge James called Father O'Malley.

Father O'Malley, who equally respected the Honorable Judge James, and having been invited by the judge to come to his chambers for coffee "because the judge was bored," dropped everything and walked the three blocks to spend time with his old friend and parishioner. Father O'Malley had been following the case very closely and with great interest for reasons of his own, so he felt a little awkward walking into the judge's chambers with his collar on after the recent testimony, which had garnered so much attention and curiosity.

Judge James's chambers were imposing because of the size and the manner in which it was furnished for business and comfort. In addition to the overhanging mahogany desk with a leather swivel chair for the judge and four matching brown leather club chairs for the attorneys, there was also a comfortable sitting area featuring an upholstered couch, two wing-back chairs, and a brass coffee table for more relaxed conversations and discussions. Judge James got up when Father O'Malley walked in, out of respect, and the two of them made themselves at home in the wing-back chairs to talk.

There was no mystery as to the reason for the meeting. The defendant was worth talking about, even if he were a psychopath.

"Let me ask you this, Father," Judge James asked, "Assume this was a movie, and it sure seemed like one in that courtroom. Why wouldn't this agent of Satan in human form just disappear versus sitting in prison and going through a trial?"

"I'll tell you why, since you asked," the father answered without hesitation. "First of all, I'm not convinced this *was* a movie . . . but whether it was or not, my answer's the same."

Judge James moved closer to his priest, for over the years, his hearing was beginning to wane, and he didn't want to miss a word.

"Sitting in prison for someone who lives in hell is like being on a vacation, you agree?"

The judge nodded in agreement.

"The reason he didn't just disappear, which he could do at any time, would be . . . or was . . . to have a forum. This case is receiving international attention . . . and he would have known and wanted that to be so . . . in order that his message could be communicated to the ends of the earth. Joe, this defendant had an agenda, and I think he pulled it off." To the judge, Father O'Malley sounded awfully certain about his opinion.

"Are you telling me," the judge asked, not thinking of the trial as a movie at this moment, "that you actually believe this guy is from another world?"

"I believe he is indeed an agent from hell," Father O'Malley answered, "And God was in accord with his message: sick of the evil in the world."

* * *

Every day, the defendant would be brought to the tenth floor of the federal courthouse in handcuffs and shackles and locked in a prison cell down a hallway from the marshal's main office. He also had to be immediately available in case there was a jury question or a verdict, for the court and the jury were not to wait for transport from Dauphin County Prison. Once in the cell, shackles would be removed but not handcuffs. His waiting area was ten feet square. Three of the walls were constructed of concrete and the fourth of solid steel bars. There was an iron cot and a toilet . . . and that was it. The defendant would be fed by handing him a bag through the bars.

He had sent a message to Yvette Lewis through Carlucci that he wanted to see her. He did not expect a response . . . but he was wrong.

On the fifth day of deliberations, a marshal escorted her down the hallway to the defendant's cell, and the marshal's parting instruction was to stay three feet from the steel bars. She had come alone and had not told Spokane or Yoder that she was going to do this.

"Hello," she said affably.

"Thank you for coming," he answered.

"Why the invitation?" she asked.

"I just wanted to apologize if I scared you last time we met. I just didn't want you getting close to me."

"Thanks for the apology," she said, "because you really scared the shit out of me that day."

"I know," he answered somewhat pensively.

"Can I ask you something?" she asked.

"You want to know how I knew about Jimmy," he responded.

"Exactly."

WILLIAM C. COSTOPOULOS

"I saw you in court during my testimony," he answered, "If you believe that I am who I say I am . . . that's your answer."

"And if I don't?"

"Then," he responded, "There is no answer . . . but having said that, you will believe that I am who I say I am soon enough."

"When?"

"Soon," he answered smiling. "In addition to apologizing to you, I just want to say good-bye and thank you for trying to help me earlier."

"Is that it?"

"That's it," he said, and with those final words, whoever this being was lowered his gaze, signaling that the meeting was over.

* * *

On the sixth day of deliberations, the jury had a question that was written out on a note and hand-delivered to the judge's chambers.

The judge, as required by law, summoned all the lawyers into his chambers to have the question read to the stenographer for the record.

Nelson and Korsakov were in chambers for the government.

Carlucci and Jackson were present for the defense.

"Counsel," the judge said, "The jury has a question that I'll read into the record, and thereafter, I'll tell you how I'm going to answer it.

"For the record," he said, looking straight at the stenographer, "The question of the jury, verbatim, is 'The defendant states that Fran Korsakov met with the DNA expert in Quantico without telling Mr. Nelson. Did Fran Korsakov meet with the DNA expert in Quantico? If he did, had he told Mr. Nelson? And how did the defendant know this?'

"That's the question, counsel," Judge James stated.

Nelson scowled at Korsakov.

Carlucci smiled at Jackson ever so slightly.

"I'm not going to make a media event out of this," Judge James stated, "So I'm going to send word to them that we cannot supplement the record, and they can only consider that which they heard in the courtroom and decide for themselves. Their deliberations must be based on the testimony they heard, and they can consider whether the alleged meeting between Korsakov and the DNA expert took place and whether Korsakov had notified Nelson about it. The jury is also to consider whether these allegations made by the defendant were refuted by the government. Any questions, counsel?"

"Do you have to add that they can consider whether the defendant's allegations about me were refuted by the government?" Korsakov asked, audibly distraught.

"I don't know if I have to, but I'm going to," Judge James answered, and that ended any further dialogue.

* * *

On the seventh day of deliberations, the jury sent word to the Honorable Judge James that they were deadlocked.

Judge James directed his tipstaff to bring counsel to the courtroom immediately.

The jury filed into the jury box, and there was no doubt about it . . . They were indeed deadlocked.

The gallery and the world outside waited with bated breath.

Three marshals rushed down the hallway to get the defendant and take him to the courtroom for the jury's announcement.

The steel cell door was securely in place. The handcuffs of the defendant had been laid on the cot, still clasped together.

He was gone.

CHAPTER 22

MORTALITY

TEN YEARS HAD passed since the defendant . . . or agent of Satan . . . disappeared.

There are those mortal souls who will never believe in heaven or hell, and they are convinced the defendant escaped, and the United States government was too embarrassed to admit it.

The three United States marshals knew better. The steel cell door was impenetrable and secured, the handcuffs on the defendant were not designed for a magic show, and the defendant would have had to sneak past all three of them at the front desk, which was the only way out.

And that didn't happen.

Nevertheless, there was a far-reaching search that extended to all four corners of the earth, and the defendant was put on the FBI's ten most wanted list, complete with his picture in print everywhere.

The result?

He was gone.

And never heard from again.

* * *

Time marches on for all of us, the living.

And ten years here on earth is a long time . . . at least relatively speaking.

Sam Nelson, former United States attorney for the Middle District, retired at the age of sixty, and that hung jury in Harrisburg was the last case he ever tried. He stays at home with his beloved wife and enjoys his grandchildren. He will never forget the call he got from Quantico, Virginia, three months after the trial, advising him that Dr. Jennifer Janson had died, having passed away from an unexpected heart attack. She was only thirty-seven.

Fran Korsakov resigned as assistant United States attorney for the Middle District once that phone call came in about Janson. He never went back to the practice of law. He married the secretary, but it didn't last. He lives alone, and his hair, by the way, is completely white.

Frank Carlucci went into private practice and is doing very well. He and his wife are still married, with children who are now in college.

Prof. Stephanie Jackson continued to teach criminal law and procedure; she transferred to Penn State Dickinson School of Law at State College, Pennsylvania. She has written three books.

John Rivero went on to become a United States senator, Republican, from the great state of New York. His secret search team after the "John Doe" trial found that cell on West Eighty-First Street within a month of his hearing about it, so he was able to thwart a bombing of New York City's transit system as a result.

The FSB agent who was in the courtroom defected to America and currently attends the Greek Orthodox Church in Camp Hill, Pennsylvania.

Liam Spokane continued as director of counterintelligence for eight years, under two more presidents, and retired with distinction and honor.

George Yoder is still there but wears eyeglasses now that are very thick.

Yvette Lewis remained happily married, and their son Jimmy at fifteen is preparing for college. She left her position as a computer technician for counterintelligence in order to spend more time with her family.

The Honorable Judge Joseph James passed away at the age of seventy-nine. His funeral was held at St. Patrick's Cathedral on State Street and was well attended. The service was presided over by Fr. Michael O'Malley.

For a time after the defendant's testimony, who professed to be an agent of Satan, the acts of terrorism throughout the world diminished in frequency. The speculation was that the world had become a better place in which to live.

EPILOGUE

Ten years later

EIGHT MEN BELIEVED to be Palestinians stormed the synagogue, attacking worshippers with meat cleavers and long knives before they escaped the sacred place of worship. They came out of nowhere, screaming, "Death is upon you!" slaughtering many who were still on their knees in prayer. It was merciless and senseless and brutal.

The blood of the forty-nine victims, which included seventeen small children, crept slowly under the main door and down the steps and onto the streets of Jerusalem. Some of the victims were beheaded; all the victims were unarmed. Eight people were also wounded in the attack, including two police officers. Four of the wounded were in serious condition; one was an eight-year-old child who had lost an arm.

A renowned Chicago rabbi and two American graduate students were among the dead. The rabbi was a principal philosopher and founder of the modern Orthodox movement, according to the *Jerusalem Post*. The students were from Boston, majoring in religion at Yale University and touring the Holy Land for a semester's credit. This all happened during the week of Passover, the most holy week for the Jewish world, in April 2026.

This act of terrorism brought an immediate response from the United States secretary of state, who denounced it as an "act of pure terror and senseless brutality." The *New York Times* reported that the attack was the deadliest in Jerusalem in years and was bound to ratchet up fears of sustained violence in the city, already on edge amid soaring tensions over a contested holy site.

Outside the synagogue, thousands of people were on the streets weeping and screaming, consumed with grief. Many were on their knees with their heads bowed in prayer asking for guidance and the strength to carry on. This was not an act of God but one of the great evils denounced in the Bible, for it was in the Ten Commandments that the taking of life was the greatest wrong that could be committed by mankind.

The man did not appear to be distressed, nor was he on his knees in prayer. One would guess him to be British. He was dressed in blue jeans, leather boots, a white shirt open at the collar, and a silk jacket and looked to be in his midforties. His hair was dark, graying at the temples, and swept back. His picture and profile was on the FBI's most wanted list, and he had been considered a fugitive from justice since the trial in America. Though ten years had passed since that trial, his face had not aged at all.

Standing there, amid the pandemonium and ghastly consequences of yet another mortal act of inexpressible evil, he watched.

AUTHOR'S NOTE

THIS STORY IS a novel based on the world we live in. Its references to terrorism are based on some events that actually happened, and many of today's readers have lived through them. Sometimes the lines get blurred between what is real and what is not, but it's a novel and not based on a true story.

That's it for my disclaimer.

If this were a movie, it would not be for children.

If this were a movie, the adult audiences would be warned that horrific events were about to be depicted on the screen. Sadly, I'm not sure that such a warning would be necessary today because the visual of terror and violence is an unfortunate part of our daily lives. The setting for this story was set in America, but it could easily have taken place in Pakistan, Afghanistan, Iran, Iraq, or London. Many other countries in the world have witnessed firsthand these senseless acts of brutality. Television and computer screens bring man's barbaric depravity into our homes as they are happening, live and in color. Today's indescribable evil is now digitized.

We have come a long way since Adam and Eve.

But there is only one ending.